"Keep It In Knickers"

Adventure, travel, affairs, flings, love, heartbreak –
It's all on offer, when you're...

Fifty and Fabulous

J R Sanders

www.jrsanders.com.au

'Keep It In Yor Knickers'

A copy of this publication can be found in the National Library
of Australia.

ISBN: 9781742840697 (pbk.)

Published by Book Pal
www.bookpal.com.au

For Joyce and Brian
I hope you're not too embarrassed!

Acknowledgements

Given that this is my first novel and it was kept a secret from almost everyone, my list is short but indeed worthy.

Firstly, my eternal gratitude to Pauline Gordon, a stranger I met in a chance meeting in a café in Hastings UK, for listening to my crazy idea for a book. Thank you for giving me the push to get started - "just tell your story like you're emailing to your friends" - I did just that. You got me over my first hurdle.

To Martin and Lin Rogers, your enthusiasm and willingness to mentor me is humbling. Thank you so much for helping me 'put it out there'.

My cover designer Josh Ali, your artwork is amazing! You took an idea from my mind and translated it exactly as I imagined it - and then some. I'll be forever grateful to you for creating such a stunning, standout cover for me. Your talent is just brilliant!

Susannah and Sharon, my very dear friends in the UK, your encouragement has been overwhelming. Love that you're loving my journey. Thank you for being my first critiques, and for still talking to me even after you'd read it.

My long time friend John Zac - thank you for believing in me. You got me over my last hurdle.

To my two daughters - a heartfelt thank you for growing into two beautiful, sensible young ladies.

This may not be quite what you expected for my first novel, but I know you'll be proud of me anyway.

Finally, it would be remiss of me not to thank George. Without him I wouldn't have had a story to tell. So thank you from the bottom of my heart. For the fun times, the adventures, the laughs, the experience. It was quite a ride!

And a huge thank you to the universe for bringing all these people into my life at just the right time. I truly am blessed!

Contents

Chapter 1

It's Raining Men

For an Easter break this was an unseasonably fine
one. Clear sunny days and balmy nights, this was to
be a weekend to remember with the new man in my
life, Russell. Easter on the Gold Coast is traditionally
wet - all those poor campers on Frazer Island - I can
never understand why they chance it.

He had booked an apartment in the heart of
Broadbeach, above the 'café' strip. Lazing by the
pool, walks along the beach, dinner at wonderful
restaurants were the plans. Russell had gone to a lot
of bother to impress me - flowers on arrival, champagne on ice, strawberries at the ready. We both
flittered about preparing canapés and setting out the
table on the balcony, both nervously waiting for our
guest to announce his arrival. The butterflies in my
stomach were trying out for the Red Arrows, I was
sure. So I opened the champagne and downed a glass
while Russell puffed on a cigarette in the next room
thinking I wouldn't know what he was doing. He
had described himself as a non-smoker, but he was
far from that. I'd broken my own rule and continued
to date him even after I knew he smoked. He had
other lovely qualities, I told myself. Hmmm, more
about that later.

I went to the loo, yet again. I fixed my hair and lipstick, yet again. Another swig of champagne, yet again.

The internal phone rang, then the knock at the door. Not a shy, hesitant tap, but a confidant full tune rat a tat tat. I opened the door with mixed feelings of trepidation and excitement and in came George. Or perhaps 'in blew George' would be more apt. I had geared myself up for a creepy, sleazy not very good looking man with a face only a mother could love, much older and with no style whatsoever. What presented before me was a good looking, clean shaven slightly balding man in stylish clothes and a cheeky smile that could melt hearts. And full of confidence and cheerfulness.

The intro's were made and I ushered the three of us out to the balcony. Russell was the perfect host, serving champagne to me and George and a beer for himself. The nibbles were bought out and we settled down to some light hearted banter. Turns out George and I had quite a lot in common - he had completed quite a few renovating jobs in the area that I lived and worked, so we knew a few people in common. He also knew the area in Sydney I had been bought up in, which impressed me considering he was from England.

He told a few jokes and we all relaxed and laughed and drank till the bottle was emptied. The butterflies had called it a day by this stage and I was pleasantly surprised at how comfortable I was feeling with this guy. I have to say I was actually looking forward to what was on the agenda.

What I need to mention here is that Russell was into all things kinky (a common trend among middle age men, I was to discover - sadly for some it seemed to be the only way they could manage arousal). After a (thankfully) failed attempt at meeting up with a couple for a spot of swinging, we had agreed to invite George over for a bit of a threesome. From a purely selfish point of view, I was gladly up for it - if he was nice, as the pleasure was to be all mine, so to speak! Shock, horror I hear you say! Well, having experienced it a couple of times before, I'm here to tell you it is very nice if it's done sensitively. A couple of times before? What? That's another story I won't go into. Suffice to say that in my new found adventurous phase, I thoroughly enjoyed it.

Sufficiently heady from the numerous glasses of champagne, I coerced the two men into the bedroom. This was going to be fun, I'd decided in my slightly inebriated state.

And so we began, undressing each other seductively. Kissing, fondling and more kissing led to us finally making our way onto the bed to partake in some serious lovemaking. All was going well and I was enjoying the attention, when Russell suddenly had a hissy fit and left the room ranting about how we could just get on with it ourselves, it was just sex after all, and he was going to have a cigarette and a drink.

So we did! George and I had really clicked and were thoroughly enjoying the intimacy. Of course, I did go out to see Russell and he was quite okay about us continuing, he just wasn't 'up' to it. Oh well, his problem I thought to myself. He's the one that set this all up, and damned if I was going to let one of his moods spoil my enjoyment.

This selfish attitude of mine, I was discovering, was a product of the new 'fifty something' woman who has discovered that after a lifetime of pandering to husbands and raising children, she has adopted an 'it's all about me' attitude. Here, here - about time, I hear you say!

So, George and I continued having sex - very nice sex I might add. And whispered sweet nothings to each other. Well, not exactly sweet nothings - more "I think you're lovely and really want to see you again", and my responding with "so do I." Sensing that Russell was clearly feeling left out and a bit foolish, we agreed it was probably best if George was on his way. As we both dressed, I managed to slip my business card into his trouser pocket and mouthed "call me" to him as we said our goodbyes. I had no idea then just what that tiny act of giving my number out was going to entail. I was about to begin the biggest adventure of my life.

Let's go back to the beginning. Well, not *the* beginning but where my new sexual discovery began. It was a few months before my fiftieth birthday. I had been working in an office with a 'business partner' as we classified our relationship to simplify it. In reality we were just work colleagues who got on incredibly well with each other and worked to each other's strengths, so had teamed up together as a partnership. He was happily married, I knew his wife really well and we all got along fine and made a lot of money together in our joint partnership. Rumours were rife of course that we were lovers, I always joked that I was his 'day wife' and got the best part of him, his 'night' wife getting the tired grumpy leftovers at the end of the day.

We had a wonderful time together and I'll be forever thankful to him, for apart from enabling me to earn more money than I'd ever imagined, he most importantly built up my self esteem, convincing me that as my confidence in my work capabilities grew, so did my sexuality. I'd been on my own for five years and had only recently had my first sexual encounter, with a client who had pursued me - a much younger man - and that certainly made me feel good about myself. Another self imposed rule I had broken - never get involved with a client. Especially where I lived, everybody gossiped. Mind you, I never heard from him again after that one encounter! I must have frightened the life out of him.

As I approached my big 5 0 day, I realised that this was the first time in my life that I'd ever *really* felt sexy. Married at nineteen to a man I'd been with since I was sweet sixteen (and my first and only sexual partner), I spent the next 25 years being a wife and mother, working and keeping house like a good wife did. Only now that my girls were young women with their own lives and partners, and divorced after 25 years of marriage, I had the freedom to do whatever I wanted with no one to answer to. And I looked the best I'd looked in years. It is a strange phenomenon, this new 50's woman. I heard someone once say it's like we've done a full circle and are now interested in boys again!

So, with my new found confidence and freedom, I set out making up for lost time as they say. Not really sure what sparked it off but I suddenly realised I'd missed out on a lot of fun and experience in my life, especially sexually. Not that I had any regrets about my faithful marriage - that was something of a rarity that I was proud of - but I just realised that there would be no accolades at my funeral for being the only woman to have only had one man in her life!

Over a period of about four months from my birthday which falls just before Christmas, I embarked on what could only be described as a 'feeding frenzy' of men. I pretty much shagged every bloke that glanced my way. Well, maybe that's a bit of an exaggeration, but suffice to say I quelled my desire. All met via the internet, I didn't discriminate - if they were interested, so was I. Some were young (very young, I'm embarrassed to say), I knew they were just wanting the experience of being with an older woman to satisfy their fetish, but I was happy to have bragging rights as well. I was really surprised to find just how many young men fantasize about sex with an older woman. And I was willing to let them find out. I actually flew to Sydney one weekend to meet up with a young man who had been emailing me the most sensual messages - good enough for a book I thought. Spent the night with him, taught him a few things then sent him off to uni the next morning, while I enjoyed the harbour and Watson's

Bay for the day before flying home. I was clearly up for anything!

They say that men and women give off phero-mones when they are 'available and looking'. Well, I must have been emitting huge doses of the stuff, because men were coming out of the woodwork. I had been on the beach less than ten minutes one day, and was just setting myself up and putting sunscreen on. Suddenly this young guy from a few metres away plops down beside me and offers to put some lotion on my back where I couldn't reach. Before I knew it, his hands had wandered round to my breasts with him muttering how he'd like to get to know me and them a little closer! I was loving this! We arranged a date for later in the week, had a nice dinner and then sex in his car. Poor guy was so excited that it was all over before it began - if you know what I mean. He was really embarrassed - I went on to learn that this is a common problem with younger men when they encounter an older woman.

My sexual encounters were the subject of great enjoyment at my local hairdressers - to the point where I would actually be cornered as I walked past the salon, for the latest update. My stories were always received with great expectation, some were so absurd they were hard to believe. Like the time I flew to Melbourne to meet up with Riley, a gorgeous black man who'd been sending me love notes. We were to drive along the Great Ocean Road, I was so looking forward to this long weekend, it was to be very romantic. Guess what? He was a no show at the airport! How stupid and angry did I feel! I had foolishly not even thought about getting a phone number from him - he had mine - so was left stranded. Serves you right I hear you say - yes, I deserved that. Luckily for me I had checked out a couple of cheap hotels prior to leaving, just in case it didn't work out with him, so I took myself off to one for the night and flew home the next day. Ah, you live and learn. And laugh. All part of the adventure.

The most memorable and unbelievable encounter was with a man I met up with for dinner, who was in town for just the weekend. We had chatted on the internet all afternoon, he seemed pleasant enough and really just wanted some company for dinner. I thought, why not? What have I got to lose? Certainly not my virginity if it goes that far! So I headed into town to meet him. We had a delightful dinner and he told me the most amazing story that to this day I don't know how much of is true. He was a paramedic (Australian) based in New York who had been the second man in to the first Twin Towers building on that fateful day. Many of his colleagues never came out of the building, also the only woman he'd been in a relationship with in nineteen years since his divorce was lost in the tragedy. How do you respond to that? I didn't, I just let him talk. As if to confirm his story, he showed me his uniform back in his hotel, along with a jacket which was a kind of bikie type with an emblem on the back, that he'd been presented with for his efforts as a rescuer. He also had a ring specially presented to him from the President, and numerous medals and badges. As this was only four years since the event, I had to believe that all this was the genuine article - who would replicate this kind of stuff so soon after such a horrendous event? That would be just sick, I told myself.

He was over here on leave and treatment for a thyroid problem that had flared up since the tragedy. He also part owned and managed a travel agency in the U.S. that specialized in coach trips - I was able to verify this as he took me to Sea World the next afternoon, and was able to get me entry at a huge discount after showing his travel agency badge and having a word to the manager. The next piece of the puzzle to this curious man was that he was heir to a title in Scotland! Now I had no way of proving this story, but apparently he was the sole surviving relative of a Laird of a manor in Scotland. He was heading over to England in April to receive his title - a Lordship if you please - from none other than the Queen. A month or so after we met he emailed me asking if I had a current passport and could I be on standby to accompany him! Well, I did fancy myself as a lady of the manor! He had treated me like a princess that weekend, had bought expensive bath and massage oils and candles for me and spoilt me incredibly. Also taught me a few tricks I hadn't known about. Well, he was a paramedic and knew a bit about anatomy he explained to me. We had an amazing time and I really grew quite fond of him.

When he left to return to the U.S., we emailed a few times. He was a military Paramedic and was being sent to Iraq. On one occasion I had emailed to one of his addresses (he used a few different ones), and received a reply from a fellow named Michael who explained that he was his 'Aide de Campe', who screened all his incoming mail before allowing him to read it! My god, who *was* this man I'd dated? I joked with Michael and said I was so glad I hadn't sent anything saucy to Rex. I don't think Michael would have minded somehow, judging from his comments. Rex and I met up again some months later when he was again sent home for leave from Iraq, but he became ill with his thyroid again and was waiting for a date for hospital. Last I heard of him he was being posted to Guam.

It did make for the most fascinating story at the time - my friends couldn't wait for the next installment. As I said, I don't know how much of it was true, but he did me no harm. Rex was a thorough gentleman to me, big and cuddly like a bear. With the smallest penis I've ever seen in my life. Ah well, its not the quantity, it's the quality. So they say.

During my foray's with this gentle giant, I met Russell. He lived up in Brisbane, in a high rise apartment on the river. A beautiful spot, I drove up there regularly to stay as it was a lovely break for me. Our relationship lasted six weeks, he had fallen for me big time but I wasn't so sure. Something just wasn't quite right. He would have mood swings for no apparent reason - huge black mood swings. One night I actually feared for my life, his mood was so dark. He had offered me a ring (which belonged to an old girlfriend!) and I rejected it. I wasn't ready for that kind of commitment - it was ringing 'I own you now' alarm bells in my head. And his preference for all things kinky was warning me off. He could only perform if I wore sexy gear and talked dirty to him. I mean, really, if I've got to do that every time I want sex, why bother! I don't mind the occasional kinky session, but every time? No thank you.

I had confided in a very close friend about this dark side of him - thank god I did. Turns out she was right. Her advice was to get out now, he's a manic depressive and it would just get worse. She'd been married to one - he would end up beating me, she warned. So after that night I began my break up with Russell. This wasn't going to be an easy break up, he hounded me for three months before it finally ended. I was a little concerned about him, you hear of men doing awful things when they've been dumped. As one very cynical friend put it - at least his contact with you shows he hasn't thrown himself off his balcony yet! He did live on the 20th floor - she had a point.

These romantic episodes were a welcome distraction from my working life which had gone down the toilet since my fiftieth birthday. The office I had worked in had been sold and I didn't wish to stay on. My business partner took off up the coast and opened an office there. I started at a previous colleague's new office he had taken over, but it was going nowhere. I stayed on for three months but hardly made a dollar. My previous boss offered me the role of manager of a new office he had commenced in a different area, so I took the position. That year was particularly unsettling, I didn't earn much money and there certainly were no overseas trips in that twelve month period. I could barely make ends meet. And here I was with a new mortgage to manage - it was pretty stressful I have to say.

Thank goodness George came into my life when he did.

Chapter 2

Afterglow

"Hi, it's George here. I'm workin in Broadbeach this week. Would you like to meet up for a laugh an' some fun?" my text message read from an unknown number.

"I'm still seeing Russell, but what the heck - yes I'd love to" I replied.

"Georges, Sanctuary Cove wed at 1?"

"See you then. Looking forward to it" I replied.

"Oh, do you prefer red or white? And I'm not referring to wine!" I P S'd to him.

"White for day time. Mmm, thx" George replied.

And so it began. How was I to know I was in for the roller coaster ride of my life?

I should point out here one important fact, just so you get the picture. This man is a part time comedian - a very good one who'd been doing the circuit in Australia and the UK for around ten years as a support to the big names. Carpenter by day, funny man on tap. All the more funnier because of his broad Yorkshire accent that us Aussies have trouble understanding.

I wore my 'Paris' dress as I called it. Black and white print, a V neck showing just enough cleavage to tantalise, and a full swirly skirt nipped in at the waist with a black sash. I felt like I was in Paris when

I wore it - very French. Oh, and a gorgeous white bra and matching knickers with little silver beads all over them. I'd bought the set in a market in Italy last year on my surprise visit to my friend in Arma di Taggia. Cost five euros and looked like a million dollars.

We were sat at a table by the window overlooking the Marina, the food and the service were impeccable as always. I've never had a bad meal at that restaurant, I can honestly say. We both couldn't believe how comfortable we felt with each other, it was like we'd known each other for ever. We laughed, he joked, I laughed at his jokes - the banter was free flowing. The young couple beside us joined in, they were on a first date (so were we, kind of - sex first, then a date - how unconventional). He kept them amused, telling them we'd met in prison - he was my probation officer and this was all part of the job. We took photos of them, they took photos of us - she worked for the local newspaper - said she would publish them in the weekend issue, much to our horror! We both had reason to hope she was joking.

"So, have you got time to come back to my place?" I questioned.

"I thought you'd never ask", "'cause I have, the afternoon's all yours gorgeous".

Barely making it up the stairs before we were in each other's arms, the kisses were passionate. And fantastic. I'd never been kissed like this before I'm sure. His tongue explored every corner of my mouth, and mine his. He tasted divine. Sadly I'd never enjoyed kissing when I was married, my husband had been a smoker all his life and it had turned me off kissing forever. Until now.

George unzipped my dress - this was a little tricky as it was a side zipper, I had to point out. It fell to the floor. I undid his shirt and belt and removed his pants, all very seductively. And all the while our lips never parted. No underpants - I do like a man who comes prepared, I commented.

"You do look rather silly standing there in nothing but your shoes and socks and an enormous erection" I giggled. With that he swung his cock from side to side.

"Just doin' my warm up exercises" he retorted as he kicked off his shoes and flung the socks across the room. My gorgeous bra and knickers lasted all of a minute before they were off as well - why do we women bother with sexy underwear? They never even notice it, its off before you can blink. Let alone making a few seductive poses for their enjoyment. Glad I hadn't paid a fortune, I thought to myself.

Our lovemaking began at the foot of the bed, still standing. My first orgasm happened almost spontaneously, this man really turned me on. And knew how to turn me on. We made our way onto the bed, where I had placed a beautiful white towel (compliments of the Versace hotel), as we lay locked together in each others arms. He looked quizzically at me.

"There's something I need to let you know" I started.

"I have multiple orgasms" I confessed.

"Wow! I'm gonna enjoy *this*. Like how many?"

"Lots" I answered.

We made love on and off for about three hours. It was fantastic. No hindrances like last time. We just let ourselves go, completely un-inhibited. Finally, I conceded defeat, exhausted.

"I think I'm done" I muttered contentedly as I fell back into the pillow.

"Jesus, when you said multiple orgasms, I didn't realize you meant multiples of ten!" George gasped. "Christ, I wish I had your stamina. I wish I could come a quarter of the times you came!" he laughed. "How many did you have?"

" I lost count after ten" I joked.

"Well, I did warn you." "Now you know what the towel's for?" I asked. He laughed.

We'd opened up about our lives completely during this session. I told him how I was having a hard time getting rid of Russell and about how I found out he was a manic depressive. "Tell him you're seeing me now" George suggested. Not a good idea, I replied. "He has your email address, who knows what he might do".

"Yes, not a good idea, scrap that suggestion."

George told me he was married. Ohhh, I hear you groan.

It didn't bother me, I'd half suspected it anyway. It wasn't the first married man I'd been with. To be quite honest, it suited me just fine.

After the obsessive, possessive nature of my relationship with Russell - he wanted to know what I was doing and who I was with every hour of the day

- I had decided that a married man was a much better proposition.

No demands on me, no getting too clingy, no wanting to know my every move.

Just good clean sex. Which was all I wanted really. I had a perfectly wonderful lifestyle with a great circle of friends, travelled when I wanted and wasn't prepared to give up my independence at this stage of my life.

So his honesty was actually quite refreshing, and appealing. Married for only a year, his second marriage. His first had lasted over twenty years and had produced one daughter who was his princess as I was to find out. He'd met this new wife on a holiday in Portugal not long after his divorce. Still living in England at the time. A holiday romance - the usual story. Had a beach wedding here in Australia two years later and been living here since. He admitted he had married on a whim and had never really 'fallen in love' with her. But admired her and they got on very well. He just wasn't happy. Well, when one strays after only a year of marriage, something's definitely not right is it? I took it all in, reserved my judgement and decided what the hell! I really like this guy, he's great fun to be with, a fantastic lover and its his problem he's got to deal with. Not mine.

If it wasn't me he was playing around with, it would be someone else. And there probably was other 'someone else's' for all I knew. It didn't matter to me.

I enjoyed him. He made me laugh. That was important to me. And he was well hung. That was important to me too.

We started seeing more of each other. I was lucky I had a job that I could take time out whenever it suited me, with no questions asked. No one had to know what I was up to during my days. Well, except for the tell tale afterglow that women wear when they've had sex - how come other women can pick it a mile off?

"You look like the cat that got the cream" one of my friends commented one evening after a session with George.

"You've had sex today haven't you?"

"Gosh, is it that obvious!" I blurted back to her.

"Afraid so, you lucky bitch! That comedian fellow again?"

"Yes, and my stomach's aching from laughing so much again."

" Better than your fanny aching, hey?" Di replied.

"Oh, that's aching too. But that's a nice pain!" I laughed.

We enjoyed a couple of wines and had a good laugh as I recounted some of the afternoon's jokes George had told me.

The weeks went on and the internet dating petered out. Although, it was during this time that the Lord Rex and his Aide de Campe episode came and went; and the 'no-show' Riley weekend happened. I was able to recall all of this to George, he thought it was hilarious. Oh, and 'mad mood' Russell finally dropped out of my life. Work was taking up a lot of my time and I was quite content with my liaisons with George to keep me satisfied. I have to say, even though he was 'stealing' time out of his working day too, he never rushed things. I was never made to feel like he was on a time limit with me before rushing home. He was always very attentive and stayed until I was ready for him to go. Usually as I lay exhausted on the bed with that euphoric look on my face that told him his job was done!

I invited George to the opening of a new office I was heading up back in my old stomping ground. Angie, my friend and business partner in this venture decided that a grand opening 'Cocktail Party' would be appropriate to generate new business and let the locals know I was back. Fortunately, I had built up a respected network of clients in the community who were all delighted that I was taking charge of this new office.

The evening was a huge success. I introduced George as a 'friend'; some of the people knew he was married so we kept our relationship very discreet. He ended up making the introductory speech and was a huge hit with the guests. A few of them asked if we were married - "you two look like you belong to each other, you look great together" was one comment. Admittedly, we did look an item together. You know how some couples just look right? Yet others look so chalk and cheese you wonder how they are together. We bounced off each other with our humour. He bought out the comedic side of me that I'd been too stuffy to show up till now. It was very refreshing. I loved being with him.

He came back to my house after the party for our own 'after party', staying till quite late before heading home.

"Damn you Gorgeous George. Why did tonight have to end?" I messaged him on his way home.

"I wish it hadn't too. Yor one sexy lady you know xxxx" he replied.

"I'm in Surfers with my mate Tommy. Wanna join us for a drink? He wants you to" came a text from George one Friday night while I was out with the girls.

"I'd love to, I'll see what I can do" I messaged back. How was I going to escape from my group without offending them? "Sorry girls, but I've had a better offer"? I couldn't do that. Others could, but I couldn't. That's just rude. So I faked a headache and hightailed it into Surfers Paradise to meet up with George and his friend! That's terrible I know, but I didn't want to insult them. I raced home first and changed into something a little sexier and was down at Melba's Bar within half an hour.

Tommy was going through a marriage break-up and was feeling a little sorry for himself. He'd been wanting to meet me, he'd seen me briefly one day when I stopped by a worksite they were on. Did he have visions of having a piece of me himself? I don't know - maybe. Given the circumstances of my relationship with his mate, he probably thought I'd be up for it. I wasn't. He confided in me that George never stops talking about me when they're at work, and that he's quite smitten by me. Well that's nice, I thought. Not much good to either of us, but nice just the same.

As the night wore on I managed to cheer Tommy up a bit (with my infinite wisdom and worldly experience on matters relating to marriage break-ups I expect) and we had some good laughs and ended up in a dance club.

"Your woman is top shelf" I heard Tommy comment to George.

"What's top shelf mean?" I asked.

"It means your classy" George replied. He smiled his agreeance at Tommy. I felt good. Never before had I had this feeling of confidence and sexiness, and I was loving it.

George and I bade our goodbyes to Tommy and left him on his own. How do mates just do that to each other? Girlfriends would never do that, I mused.

"We're heading off to the beach for a bit of canoodling", George told him.

"Can't I watch?" asked Tommy.

He looked shattered. I felt sorry for him. Not about the wanting to watch us, just about how he was feeling and how his mate rubs it in his face. Men, they are so insensitive.

We did do some 'canoodling' on the beach. It was hilarious - there was a spotlight that scanned that part of the beach we had perched on, so we had to stop what we were doing every thirty seconds till the search light passed. It felt like we were in a prison camp trying to escape! It was like 'speed fondling', a new take on speed dating. We ended up collapsing on the sand laughing. Not the most romantic of scenes.

Angie and I had enrolled in one of those motivational weekends that are meant to boost your self esteem and thus your ego in six easy modules. We headed up to Brisbane and booked ourselves into a nearby hotel. The first session saw us herded into a room with the speaker prattling on about how much fun we were going to have over the course of the weekend. The second part of that session consisted of him asking us if we were having fun yet? Doing what? Nothing had started. Oh, I get it. Sitting in a room full of complete strangers all in bewildered expectation of the unknown *is* fun. How could I not know this? It was perfectly clear to the dozens of other 'enrolee's' who were screeching out "yeah's" and "whoo hoo's" to our revered speaker. Sadly, Angie and I seemed to be the only ones who didn't 'get' it. Who weren't yet having fun. We went to a break feeling broken - and this was meant to be a motivational seminar! "What did they have that we didn't?" we pondered. "Why weren't *we* having fun yet?" we asked each other.

We both realized simultaneously - it was more a case of us having what they didn't - that is an IQ with three figures. This seminar was directed at complete morons who lack any semblance of intelligence and are happy and willing to be guided like sheep through a series of mindless suggestions on how they could improve their self esteem.

I'll tell you how to do that - go hang out with your girlfriends or your mates for a weekend. If the self esteem needs improving, they'll boost you up. If it needs lowering, they'll pull you down a peg or two. That's what friends are for. And it'll save you a wad of cash that these people try to con you into parting with to continue on your 'journey' with them.

At best it will cost you a few rounds of drinks and probably a hangover.

The bell rang to mark the start of session two. With just a glance at each other, we headed for the door. The exit door. We were out of there. With a young 'follower' hot on our heels.

"But you'll miss the next session. It's really *fun!*" we heard her little voice fading behind us, as we picked up the pace and rounded the nearest corner. Into the nearest pub for a well needed drink! We both reduced ourselves to a fit of hysterics. The rest of the weekend was spent bar hopping and exploring the riverside markets. And laughing about our failed self esteem course. Did that mean we had no self esteem? Hardly.

During our bouts of laughter, I was of course text messaging George who I knew would enjoy the funny side of our exploits. After a number of clever one liners between us, the tone changed to a more serious one.

"I know this is gonna frighten the hell out of you and you'll probably run a mile, but I can't stop thinking about you. I know this isn't supposed to happen but it has, so I'm sorry if that terrifies you" I told him after his latest text.

"I thought it was only happening to me. I'm really glad about that and no I won't run a mile"; "I can't wait to see you again" came the reply.

Uh oh! I was moving into unfamiliar territory. And it felt wonderful.

Chapter 3

Sex On The Beach

Another birthday rolled around for me. What a year I had experienced as I reflected on the happenings of the past twelve months. A career that had highs and lows; a financial situation that had its ups and downs; more one night stands and quick flings than I'd ever imagined little prim and proper me could have; and I was falling for a married man. Another one of my self imposed rules I had broken. I wasn't very good at sticking to my rules was I? Or is it true that rules are made for breaking? I consoled myself with that thought.

George couldn't make it to my birthday party - just drinks with the girls like any other Friday night actually - he was doing a comedy quiz night at his local football club. These were regular gigs, gosh how I wished I was able to attend. They would have been such fun. (There's that word again.) But really fun, like laugh out loud tummy wobbling fun. But of course I couldn't ever attend one of those nights. I was the 'other' woman wasn't I?

I did however, attend a play that he starred in at a local theatre. He was the leading man, it was about a guy going through a mid life crisis who is bored with his mundane life and decides to take himself on a holiday and have an affair. Ouch, this sounds uncomfortably familiar doesn't it? I took Angie and another friend along. He was wonderful as Dennis, had to rein in his comedic tilt a little as it was meant to be slightly serious. But the audience loved him. We threw gladioli's at him at the end of the show. Kind of like Dame Edna in reverse - she usually does the throwing.

The following week I took my two sisters and aunt along. They really enjoyed it and of course loved George. He was utterly delightful after the show, playing up to them, being witty and attentive and generally charming the pants off them. No wonder I was keen on him they commented. Shame he's married, one added. Yes, it is.

To make up for missing my birthday, he took me out to dinner the following night - a Saturday night. Bit risky I thought. But I realized that with his part time comedy, he could make up an excuse for any night out if he wanted to. We went to a favourite Japanese restaurant in Surfers Paradise, a tepanyaki bar. Always great fun if you get a good chef who can entertain the crowd. We did, and had a great meal.

It was way too far to go back to my house, so we headed down to the beach again. A much more isolated part this time. We weren't gonna have this one spoiled by some damn search light! I took a rug out of the car for us to lay on. Always knew my Singapore Airlines blanket would be useful one day! And we made love on the beach, under the moon-light. The stars were twinkling at us. It was the most romantic thing I'd ever done.

"I have something I need to tell you" George whispered in my ear.

Oh god, this isn't good I thought to myself.

"I've fallen in love with you". "I'm sorry", he added.

"I love you too" was all my choked up voice managed to get out. How pathetic.

"I've been in love with you for ages. I just couldn't be the first one to say it" I added.

"It wasn't supposed to happen was it?" I asked.

"No, but I couldn't help it" he whispered again.

"Well I'm glad about that, and I'm not sorry. I love you more than I've ever loved anyone. I've never felt this way before" I continued.

"Me neither" George replied.

And we made love again. Then held each other tight while we gazed at the stars.

Christmas Day came and went. I did my usual routine of heading down to the beach early morning for a swim in the ocean. I still never stopped enjoying the concept of swimming on Christmas morning while those in the northern hemisphere were huddled around log fires drinking egg nog. Nor the meals we had here in Australia compared to those north of the equator. Salads and loads of seafood, bought at the fish markets that morning. It really was quite a quirky tradition here in Australia. The rest of the world dines on roast turkey and ham and baked vegetables. Our Christmas day's are usually so hot and steamy that the thought of heating up the kitchen all day with a roast is just not appealing. So prawns and exotic salads it is for a lot of us.

All George and I could manage was a few carefully timed texts to each other on the day. We both wished it could be different, but I knew he couldn't see me over this period and accepted that. We settled for a few warm and fuzzy emails and text messages.

Lunch was held at my sisters' house as usual. This had apparently become a tradition somehow. They had a pool and air conditioning, so it made sense to have it there. My ex husband had flown up from Sydney to spend Christmas with us, so he came along too. It was just like old times, when we were married. We now enjoyed a quite amiable relationship, after six years of separation. All the dust had settled, along with the nastiness and bitterness that comes with divorces, so we were on quite good terms now. It was good for our girls too, to see us getting along again. No chance of a reconciliation though, we were worlds apart now. Gosh, we'd been together since I was 16 and he was 17 - we were kids then. We'd grown up into completely different people to who we once were. But it was nice to have a family Christmas.

Nick was staying at my place - on the lounge - as my daughter had a house full herself. He would normally have stayed with her, she was just around the corner from me. I have to admit it did feel a little strange having him in my house - and too bad if I had wanted George to come over during the Christmas break! That would have been awkward wouldn't it? As it turned out, I was very glad he was staying with me.

The following morning - Boxing Day - I had a call from my friend Linda. We'd been friends from teenage years - had shared life's experiences together. Got married the same year, had our first babies within months of each other, moved to the Gold Coast the same year. My best friend. She had returned from her apartment in Italy where she spent roughly eight months of the year (I was so jealous), and was spending Christmas in Sydney with her parents, as she does every year. Long divorced and only one son Joshua, she was very independent and had an enviable lifestyle.

"Hi, you beat me to it. I was going to call you shortly. Merry Christmas" I chirped down the phone to her in my usual cheery voice.

I could tell from her first "hello", that something was wrong. Very wrong. She sounded dreadful. I thought she had the flu or something.

"I've some bad news to tell you. You might want to sit down" came a shaky reply.

"Joshua passed away this morning." I thought I was hearing things.

"What? Oh god! What happened?" I could feel myself starting to shake.

" Drug overdose" she replied. "John found him just half an hour ago. I rang you straight away".

I fell apart. She fell apart. I didn't know what to say. Nor did she. But somehow I kept her talking.

"I'll come down straight away. You can't be on your own" I told her.

"No, there's no need. I'm with Mum and Dad and my sister". "I'm not on my own"

"But I want to be with you. You need your friend with you" I pleaded.

"No really. Not yet. We need to come to terms with it. I'll let you know when I need you to come. Thank you" Linda replied.

"I'll let you go. I'll call you back in a few hours. Is that ok?" I suggested.

"Yes, do that. I will be able to talk then I hope. Bye." Linda hung up.

My ex husband came down the stairs, he'd just had a shower. He saw my face. Before he could ask, I blurted out what had happened and then collapsed into a crumpled mess on the chair and sobbed. And sobbed. I shook, I hyperventilated, I was a mess.

Nick was wonderful. He hugged me, sat me down again and made me comfortable. Made a cup of tea for me and rang the girls and broke the news to them. Our oldest came straight over, she only lived around the corner. We cried together. They had grown up together, went to each other's birthday parties and playgroups together. Had spent school holidays together when he came up to visit his mother. Although we hadn't seen him for a while, he had been a part of our lives. But we knew he'd had a troubled life.

I called Linda as soon as I felt it appropriate. Got a better explanation. Yes, he had overdosed himself, he was alone after attending a Christmas party the night before. Had left his girlfriend there and went home, in a black mood apparently. Took a concoction of just six pills, knew they would do the trick. His father found him in the converted boatshed at the bottom of their garden where he lived. He was just 23.

I was absolutely devastated. Of course, that pales into insignificance when I consider how Linda and John and their families must have been suffering. But it did affect me very badly. I couldn't go to work all week, I rang Linda two and three times a day to check on her. I flew down to Sydney the day before the funeral to help with things, and just to support them all.

That first night I found out, I sent a text to George and told him what happened.

"Tell your daughter that you love her, won't you" I added to one of my texts.

"I do every day", he replied.

He was very kind and understanding. Came over as soon as I felt up to it - which wasn't till the following week. He just hugged me for what seemed an eternity. I needed that hug.

I stayed with my ex husband in Sydney the night before the funeral and he came with me of course. My girls had decided not to come. I had realized that neither of them had ever been to a funeral before so I think it frightened them. And they were both so angry with Joshua. How could he do this to his friends and family? I understood their feelings, I must admit I was feeling the same.

As funerals go, it was lovely. Of course, incredibly emotional for everyone. He had a ton of friends who were all equally devastated. I caught up with a whole group of friends from our teenage years who I hadn't seen for twenty odd years. It was an awful way to have a reunion. I was still quite a mess, but managed to accompany Linda into the church and be her rock to lean on throughout the ordeal. We flew home together that night - it was New Year's Eve. Went for a short walk along the beach near her home and then took her home and stayed with her a few days. She was exhausted.

How does a parent recover from the loss of a child? I hope I never have to find out for myself. I now look at my own relationship with my daughters and give thanks to two healthy, stable untroubled girls. And cherish every day with them.

The road to recovery for Linda was a long and continuing one. Also for her ex husband and his then wife, I don't know if any of them will ever fully recover from that loss.

Chapter 4

Spanish Toy Boys

"Hmmm, she looks tasty" George thought to himself as this blonde woman appeared ahead of him. "It's Judi! I know her, she *is* tasty!" he joked to himself. We were meeting up in the local tavern for a couple of drinks. I was wearing a skirt that had for no apparent purpose a tie belt around the waist which had become undone and was caught up around my waist. As we sat on the sofa at the tavern, George proceeded to fiddle with it and somehow before I realised it, had passed it under my top and out through the armhole. He then proceeded to pretend he was trying to help me out of it, passing it back under my top and out through my very generous cleavage, much to his own amusement. This of course, wasn't going un-noticed and before we knew it he had a couple of men offering to 'assist' him in his procedure! This kind of entertainment was something I was getting quite used to - wherever we went we seemed to attract an audience. Sometimes he would just throw me back on a sofa at the tavern or a nearby bar and pretend he was having his way with me, much to the amusement of onlookers. I was up for the fun of it though, and gave as much back when I could.

Trouble was though, often these antics happened at places where I was known - respectably known - so it came as quite a shock to some to see this side of me, hamming it up with this clown. One afternoon a girlfriend of mine who worked at a restaurant we would often have a drink in, came along with a blanket and threw it over us so we could have a cuddle and a grope! She had seated us in a corner especially, on a sofa, she thought we were hilarious.

Our relationship continued along for a few more months in much the same way. Catching up about once a week, sometimes just for a drink without the sex. We enjoyed each other's company, in or out of the bedroom.

I was planning a two week trip away to visit Linda who had gone back to Italy to her flat. I also planned on visiting Spain for the first time, Angie owned an apartment on the Costa Blanca and offered to let me stay there for free. It was less than 100 metres to the beach, so I gladly accepted her offer. My finances were doing okay and I was really concerned to see how Linda was coping. I of course asked George if he'd like to come with me (I knew he couldn't but it was a nice thought.)

About two weeks before my planned trip, George and I met up for a lovely afternoon session. He waited till we went to our favourite bar to break some news to me. He was leaving Australia. He'd accepted a job in Dubai. After three years in Australia he felt he couldn't make a go of it financially and this was an offer he couldn't refuse. He was leaving in two months. I was gutted. Would I like to live in Dubai with him, he asked.

"That would be cosy, wouldn't it? Just you, me and the wife" I replied, somewhat sarcastically.

"I'm leaving her when we get back to England. We are just not getting on any more. I won't do it here, it's better if we're back home where her family and friends are" George answered defensively.

We got a bit teary, we both knew how we felt about each other.

"Why do you have to go? I thought you loved it here" I asked.

"I do, and I love you, but I just can't seem to get ahead here. There's lots of opportunities over in Dubai for me". I knew there were, I'd been following the real estate market there and knew the building trade was booming.

So, our lovely afternoon ended on a really sad note. Heartbreak number one. What was I going to do without him in my life? I couldn't even entertain the thought.

Nor could I entertain the thought of moving to Dubai. Leaving my own career and my girls - couldn't even consider it. Could I?

My trip came around in two weeks. George drove me to the airport. My airline ticket hadn't arrived. It was meant to be at the Qantas desk for my collection. With just over two hours till my flight, I had to try and organise something. They weren't going to let me board without my ticket. Why had it not been E-ticketed? I don't know. After a couple of urgent phone calls, I found out my ticket was sitting in an office in Brisbane. Yes they could courier it over to the airport at their expense - I should think so!

The staff at the ticket counter were wonderful. Sent me away to have a drink and would page me when my ticket arrived. George was astounded at how calm I was taking this. So was I to be honest, I wasn't flustered at all. But there was no way I wasn't getting on that plane, he would not be taking me back home again, I was determined.

True to their word, the Qantas staff called for me with literally minutes to spare before boarding, spoke to check-in and rushed my suitcase through and I was on my way. Ticket in hand. Big hugs and kisses to George with promises of texting him when I got to Singapore. I was on board the plane. Had a nice treat when I boarded. I enquired with the senior staff if any of them knew my twin brother, Barry. He'd been with Qantas for nearly 30 years. One of them did, loved him in fact. That didn't surprise me, he is a bit of a dish - looks like Tom Sellick. So, she provided free champagne to me for the duration of the flight. And the lady sitting beside me, as she thought we were travelling together.

Of course, I knew that when I got home, I'd only have another month with George before he left - for good. I tried not to think about it.

I dutifully sent George a text when I stopped over in Singapore, sent him a quick email and did the same again when I arrived in Nice. Linda was catching a train from Taggia to meet me in Nice where I'd booked a hotel near the seafront for a couple of nights. Well, we didn't count on France and their love of strikes did we? No trains for two days. She couldn't get to Nice! So I spent the two days and nights on my own. I love Nice, so it wasn't really a problem for me. Just disappointing for Linda.

It was during this lone stay that my mind went into overdrive. I had had quite a few good settlements lately and was quite flush with cash. My broker (sounds posh doesn't it? Having your own broker!) had suggested I put some of this money into an investment property - to increase my 'portfolio'. Hardly a 'portfolio' I thought, I only own one property. I saw his point though.

So I started thinking about George's house. He was of course going to sell it. I'd asked him not to sign up with the local agent until I'd had a chance to see if I had any clients who were after an investment property. I'd never seen the property - well, how could I have when you think about it? So I rang him from Nice with my 'real estate agent' hat on, not my 'lover's' hat. I asked him to repeat his description of his house to me.

Got four bedrooms? "Yes"; two bathrooms? "Yes"; two living areas? "Yes"; pool? "Yes"; tiled roof? "Yes".

"You're not thinking of buying it are you?" he questioned.

"I could be" I replied.

So, we agreed on a price that he would accept with no commission payable of course, and I had a blank contract faxed over to me in Taggia and bought his house, sight unseen.

That was that! Business done! Linda thought I'd lost my mind. I never doubted her, I already knew that. But this was a business investment, the figures stacked up and I thought it was a good deal. I knew what I could rent the place out for, so was comfortable with the whole process.

The rest of the visit passed uneventfully. Well, kind of. Poor Linda, when I finally arrived in Taggia she was so starved of company that she talked non stop for three days and nights. About nothing really, just waffled. I let her though, I didn't mind. I knew she'd been having a tough time of late, coping with Joshua's loss.

I have to say though, that if I had any feelings of envy toward her romantic life in Italy, they were well and truly quashed after three days in that town. I emailed to George "I've now visited *the* most boring town on earth! Three days in a graveyard would have been more fun!" and "I couldn't help myself, when Linda commented about how there are many deaths here in the old town - I suggested they all probably died of boredom!" Oh, it was agony. There was nothing to do. Bars in Italy don't play music, so there's nothing to entice you into them. Absolutely no night life whatsoever. As much as I loved seeing my friend, I couldn't wait to be on my way to Spain.

I arrived in Barcelona to a throng of people all dressed in blue football shirts. There had been a huge soccer match that day and the fans were cramming the airport to get home. It was quite a spectacle, the Spanish do love their football. I had to catch a coach down to Benidorm, then another up to Calpe where

Angie's flat was located. It was late at night before I boarded the coach. I had tried some tapas at a nearby bar, I'd never had it before. Very nice. The coach trip was roughly seven hours, arriving in Benidorm around six in the morning. I did manage to catch some sleep in between noisy stops. I was pointed in the right direction for the bus stop I needed for my bus to Calpe. It was so early the ticket office hadn't opened yet. So I sat on the steps and waited.

After travelling all night and half of the previous day, you can imagine I looked a fright. I didn't care which was even worse. I was tired and hungry and just wanted a shower and a sleep in a bed. Finally the ticket office opened and I politely joined the queue. I say politely because that's what Australians do - we queue - politely. Not the Spanish - they queue jump! This rough looking man just barged in ahead of me. My protests fell on deaf ears - or Spanish ones I imagine. He didn't know what I was saying, he didn't speak English. Of course, why would he? I am in Spain after all, I reminded myself.

To my amused surprise, this rather cute looking young Spanish man came to my rescue. He sorted out the rude Spaniard and presented me to the ticket seller. He didn't speak English either, but he was my hero. He joined me on the bus where I managed to glean a tiny bit about him. His name was Elias, he lived in Calpe also, worked as an electrician and had a girlfriend who he'd been visiting. He was on his way home.

He insisted on helping me find Angie's flat and carried my suitcase for me. Who said chivalry was dead? Not in Spain it appears. After almost an hour of trundling my heavy case up and down the streets of Calpe, he finally relented and asked a local policia for directions. Spanish men are still as stupid as English speaking men in that regard - not asking for directions.

Finally we found the apartment building! It was one street behind his! Doh! I could have been there an hour ago, bless him. I thanked him profusely and somehow managed to relay an invitation to him and his girlfriend to dinner that evening as my way of thanking him for his help. Meet outside my building at eight, I instructed.

Angie's apartment was wonderful. Old with tired décor, but spacious and a view of the sea about eighty metres away. She and her two sisters' had inherited it after her father's death two years ago. The sisters' had no wish to visit, so Angie had it pretty much at her own disposal. She was joining me in a few days. She needed to clear out a few of her dad's possessions still, and organise some maintenance on the place. I had decided I would stay in a nearby hotel when she arrived, I didn't want to impose on her. And she had 'friends' she wanted to catch up with.

After a much needed hot shower and a bit of a nap, I headed out to explore. I was really going to enjoy it here. The beach was beautiful with the obligatory sunbeds and parasols available for hire, restaurants and bars were everywhere. Even some quite classy shops. A smattering of English pubs and a fabulous German restaurant completed the picture.

Then I discovered the seafront promenade. It was wonderful, all tiled and paved and stretched for miles along the beach right up to the Penon Ifach, the landmark of Calpe jutting into the sea. Bars and seafood restaurants all the way along it, and literally on the beach. Just a few steps down and you were on the sand. Even these very civilised timber platforms and foot wash showers to remove the sand before stepping back onto the promenade. Why couldn't they do this to our beaches back home?

I was going to love my week here.

Back to the apartment to change for dinner. I waited on a seat in front of my apartment building for Elias and his girlfriend. Half an hour went by and still no Spanish boy. He's chickened out I thought, as I stretched my legs and decided to go in search of somewhere to dine solo. Elias appeared from around the corner, alone.

"Where is your girlfriend?" I asked . Somehow he understood the question.

She had to work I think was the explanation. Or she'd dumped him. I don't know, he could have been saying anything - I didn't understand much more than uno and dos.

So we set off together for dinner. He lead me to a beautifully decorated Indian restaurant owned by his friend, after establishing that yes, I do eat Indian food.

The meal was lovely, the conversation was well, amusing to say the least. Me with my three words of Spanish (I forgot hola) and him with his six words of

English made for a very strained couple of hours I can tell you.

He was the perfect gentleman though, and even cuter now he'd shaved and dressed himself up from this morning. Did I mention he was twenty nine?
He escorted me back to my flat and of course accepted my invitation for another wine before leaving. Poor love, he switched the television on and proceeded to watch it, flicking channels to find something of interest. Not quite what I had in mind when I invited him up. Ahh, the innocence of youth!

A couple of wines and more strained conversation later, he finally made a move and kissed me. A nice kiss, not in the league of a George kiss, but nice just the same. Not sure who made the next move, but we had sex. On the sofa. Sorry Angie.

I'd had a bit to drink myself so was pretty relaxed and any concerns about George flew out the window when I was presented with a cute twenty nine year old Spaniard in his boxers! Besides, George was leaving me in five weeks, maybe never to be seen again!

And besides again, he wasn't exactly being faithful to me, was he?

Don't pass an opportunity, I told myself. Not at my age with someone his age anyway.

The next couple of days were spent exploring this lovely town. George was right, I was gonna love it here. He spent his honeymoon here (first one). I spent the afternoons on the beach, even braved it and went topless. When in Rome as they say. It felt really liberating. Haven't done that since my early twenties.

The lovely thing about European beaches is that no one cares what you look like, and no one stares. There were lots of families with young children on the beach, interspersed with topless women of all ages, shapes and sizes. What really convinced me to take my top off though was glancing down to the waters edge and seeing a woman in her late sixties with only one breast - topless! Hooray to her, I thought. So off with my top! What was I worried about, if she wasn't? Besides, my boobs were still in pretty good shape. So I'd been told on more than one occasion.

Elias joined me for dinner again the next night but I thankfully had most days to myself. More sex, not on the sofa though. Where was the mysterious girlfriend? Didn't exist?

Angie arrived on my fourth day. I introduced her to Elias, explaining he was an electrician. Next thing he's up on a step ladder fiddling with her fuse box. Chattering away to her in Spanish with her replying in short bursts.

"Did you understand what he was saying?" I asked her incredulously.

"Not a word" she replied. "I just answered si and no when I thought I needed to!"

Whatever the exchange was between them, he fixed her problem. The fuses kept blowing when more than one appliance went on. I think it just needed stronger fuses in the end. So the next day he fitted some new parts and I paid the bill by way of another free meal. And more sex. Fair deal, I thought.

I moved myself up to a lovely hotel at the top end of the beach. I just didn't want her to think I was intruding and taking advantage of her generosity. Given that Elias was now hanging around me like a lost puppy, it was probably just as well.

We popped in to see her one afternoon and I gave her a business card.

"I've found you a plumber" I stated. She gave me a look that needed no words.

"Don't ask" I said.

It's not how it sounds. He was a friend of Elias who also ran a clothing shop. We met and somehow I explained the problem in Angie's flat and he gave me his card to give to her. I was getting good at this.

Towards the end of my week, Elias had to work in another town, so I didn't see him again. I was kind of glad, he was beginning to cramp my style. I like my own company when I'm travelling, and didn't really have a need for a young man I couldn't converse with hanging around with me all day. Just for sex was fine actually.

Not to let my hairdressing friends down, I sent a text to the owner:

"If you are expecting a report on me finding a cute Spanish toy boy to keep me amused while I'm here, you won't be disappointed."

I took myself off to Terra Mitica on my last day. A theme park located near Benidorm. I was a bit disappointed actually, I'm used to the calibre of the ones on the Gold Coast and this one wasn't a patch on them. Plus, there was hardly anyone there. I was making my way to the bus stop at the end of the day and approached a man for directions. Mustafa, from Somalia was the blackest man I'd ever laid eyes on. He was again very helpful and clearly trying to chat me up so I was glad when the bus arrived. Gosh those pheromones are still working, I thought to myself.

I sent Angie a text - "do you have any use for a gorgeous Somalian named Mustafa?"

I can't remember her reply, something smug I'm sure.

My trip to Spain came to an end and I was on my way home.

My gorgeous George was there at the airport waiting for me as promised.

Took me home, showered together and I fell asleep in his arms a few hours later.

Chapter 5

Carpet Burns and Love Trees

I thought I'd better look at this house I'd bought while I was away. I organised with George to meet him there the next day while his wife was at work. I had looked it up on the internet using a site I subscribed to for checking ownership and saw a photo of the front of it. Oh my god, I thought! What have I bought! It was tiny, a ranch style with just three windows and a door across the front. I knew it only had a carport. I was starting to panic. Finally, I managed to bring up an aerial shot of the house and to my enormous relief it was an L shaped house and quite large. Phew! I relaxed again.

I was actually pleasantly surprised when I saw it. An extension had been done to it years before George bought it, the bathrooms and kitchen were in good condition and the pool was quite new and lovely. I was pleased with it. I took some photos of it so I could get it on the internet straight away to rent it out. I had a few unforeseen problems with the settlement process - it didn't value up as high as I hoped so I had to throw more of my own money at it, but it went smoothly after that. I managed to find a tenant for it within two weeks of owning it so it was no bother.

What I wasn't pleased with though was the thought that I was about to lose George out of my life. I was putting on a brave face to him but behind the mask it was tearing me apart. Of course, I wasn't going to let him see me cry.

"If I do that, then I'll have to kill you" I joked to him. Ever the strong one, I couldn't bear to let him see my weakness.

We saw as much of each other as was reasonably possible during the month before he left. We made love in all sorts of places, not just at home. One night we'd been into Surfers and went parking afterwards. We were outside the car and made love leaning up against a tree. It started raining and we just continued on. It was like the heavens were crying for us. I remember that tree and always look when I pass it on my trips down to the beach. Another afternoon we drew the blinds in the back office and had sex on the desk. I did lock the front door in case you're wondering. After we had knocked all the paperwork off the desk, we moved onto the floor. And made jokes about carpet burns.

We had sex in an empty house that I was marketing. Overlooking the canals, it was quite a grand home. Poor owner, he'll never know about that.

On what was to be our last night together, we went to the bar at the top of the Q1 tower in Broadbeach. It was very emotional, we cried in each other's arms. He walked me to my car and we said our goodbyes. I held myself together until I got under-way. I watched him as he walked down the street to his car - his friends work car actually. He'd already sold his so had a borrowed one till he left in a few days. It wasn't there! I saw him looking around, panic stricken. He came back up to me, really stressing. Someone had stolen his friends car! How was he going to explain this to his mate? I'd never seen him so stressed before. He wasn't handling it well. I guess the tension of everything was taking its toll. I calmed him down, went looking for it again and worked out a plan for him. I would take him to where he was supposed to be, and he would call the police from there. He was starting to calm a little.

"Are you sure this is where you parked it?" I asked him.

"Yes, it was half way down this street. And now its gone" he replied anxiously.

"Hang on a minute, you met me at the shops at the bottom of the building. You came from that direction" I remembered.

And so we realized, he was in the wrong street. His car was parked in the street behind this one. He was so relieved when I remembered this, we found the car exactly where he parked it and he was on his way.

I headed home too. The tears started. The sobbing started. I didn't want him gone.

I sent him a text as I drove home, still crying: "See, you really can't live without me can you?"

"No, I know that now" he replied.

We decided we could see each other briefly one last time, the day before he left. He needed to hand the keys to the house over to me. He was to come up to my house and we could have one last love-making session before he left. It didn't quite go according to plan. He rang me to say he and his wife had had a huge row, she'd realized he was planning on leaving her when they got back to England and she suspected we were having an affair. She was going to give the keys to me, not him. I couldn't do anything about it. She rang me and I arranged to meet her at the Marriott hotel. It was quite an awkward moment. I pretended I didn't know about their argument and hadn't spoken to him. I wished them both well in their new adventure and collected the keys and left.

We were both gutted. This wasn't how it was supposed to end. All we could do now was count down the months till September when I was heading back over to Spain with Angie and we could catch up for a week in Calpe. Hopefully.

The next day, he was gone. I took over ownership of his house. It was a kind of surreal time for me. He sent me a few texts over the next few weeks and some emails. They got less and less frequent as the weeks went on. I thought I had lost him. I sent an email asking him if he was okay. Yes, he replied, he'd been a slack Alice lately and was just busy with work. And yes, he was still coming to Calpe to see me for the "sex trip of a lifetime".

"I've never heard the expression slack Alice before" I replied; " I believe the Australian version is slack arse" I continued; "but I'll forgive you your shortcomings. And I'll take the 'sex trip of a lifetime' as a compliment. Others wouldn't, but they don't know you like I do" I added to my email.

And so the planning continued for a liaison in Calpe. I had booked a Mediterranean cruise with Angie earlier in the year - long before I knew George was leaving. The plan was I would then fly to Spain and have a week with George in Angie's flat then fly onto Paris to meet up with both my daughters for a driving tour around Europe. This whole trip was to be done on a tight budget now, as I had needed to contribute more to the house purchase than I first planned. I was an expert at budget holidays though, so it didn't faze me.

The weeks passed and it was time for me to fly out again. This was the first time I'd done two European trips in one year and it did concern me that it was a trip I couldn't really afford. But the cruise had long been paid for, I couldn't let my girls down and I was to have the chance to see George again. I couldn't *not* go.

Chapter 6

Comedy Cruising

Angie and I were on different flights for some reason, so I arrived in Rome a day before her. I had booked a transfer from the airport as I arrived quite late and didn't fancy using the Italian rail system late at night. It only cost me nineteen euros and was money well spent. The driver took me past some very pretty sights and the city looked like fairyland. I'd never seen Rome at night so it was a treat for me. The driver got quite shirty with me though, when I made it clear to him that I didn't want a tour of the city for an extra charge, that I just wanted to get to my hotel. I think he thought he could charm me into accepting his kind offer! Bloody Italian men! I was not in the mood for their conniving ways.

The hotel was cheap and cheerful. Close to the Stazione Centrale which was important for us to get to the port in two days time. My room was no bigger than a closet, I'd never been in a room that was taller than it was wide! It was so stuffy I had to sleep with the window wide open. This caused quite a ruckus in the early morning though - trying to convince the local pigeons that my room was not their pigeon coop - there was definitely only enough room for one of us. Yes, a couple of them actually flew into the room! So the window was shut and I suffered the stuffiness until it was time to venture out.

I had a whole day to myself, Angie wasn't arriving till late afternoon. I decided I would do the hop on - hop off bus tour of the city. I had been to Rome a few years previously on a trip with Linda, so it was all familiar to me. After lining up for over an hour in oppressive heat, a bus finally came along that had room for a few more passengers. Next bus stop - the bus stalled and the driver couldn't get it started again. After an eternity, he finally conceded defeat and offloaded us to wait for another bus. Of course, none of them had room for an extra thirty odd passengers, so they just passed us by. A fellow arrived on a vespa, tinkered with the starter motor for a millisecond and presto! The bus was back in action again. We all jostled together to get back on the bus. Unfortunately, this jostling led to a passenger having his wallet lifted from his pocket.

A bad start to the day. I alighted and rejoined the bus a couple of more times to take in a few more sights. Of course, none of the headphones actually worked so nobody had any commentary. But my main drawcard was the Colosseum. I had not had a chance to go inside it on my last visit so definitely wanted to do that this time 'round. According to the map and my memory, it was located some distance from the other landmark sights, definitely too far to walk in that heat. So, I boarded the bus to get there. To my astonishment, the driver went sailing past the bus stop even though a number of us passengers had indicated we wanted to alight. When we objected, he replied with

"It is Sunday, the bus does not stop there on Sunday"! What the?

So here we are, in Rome - the Eternal City - wanting to see its most famous landmark on the most touristy day of the week, and the tourist bus doesn't stop there because "it is Sunday"? Italian logic, you've gotta love it don't you?

So again, I didn't get to see inside the Colosseum.

And again, I'm reminded of what I don't like about Italy.

Angie arrived on schedule and we settled into our room. Same hotel, bigger room. No pigeons to argue with over territories. We traipsed around the usual places in the early evening - the Spanish Steps, Trevi Fountain, Piazza Navona etc. An early night, we were both still jetlagged. We set off early next morning for the train trip out to the port. We were excited, neither of us had been on a cruise up till now. Before boarding a shuttle to the ship, we decided to have a beer to signal the start of our Mediterranean adventure. Neither of us were beer drinkers, but it was more refreshing than wine. It was to become one of our many traditions that we adopted for each port. Twelve days of fun and adventure lay ahead of us.

The ship was huge! And beautiful. And weird! The décor had been designed by an Italian decorator. It was such a garish collection of contradicting styles, we decided that he had had a nervous breakdown half way through his contract, but they kept him on regardless. She was fairly new, I think it was only her fourth voyage. Our room was impressive to say the least. It was better than we both expected. We apparently had scored the handicapped room, so our bathroom was quite spacious. A fact we were later to regret knowing, as the couple next door caught a glimpse of our bathroom and commented on its spaciousness compared to theirs. Hubby was quite a large man in a wheelchair, so we felt quite guilty about our good fortune for oh, about a second.

We claimed which bed we would have - a decision made simple by Angie dumping her heavy suitcase on the nearest bed she came to. Unpacking took no time. I took up a tiny part of one side of the bathroom vanity, Angie's collection spread through the other side and out onto the dressing table area in the cabin. I'm a neat freak. Angie is, well, quite the opposite. This was going to be a test of both our resolves. I do know that neat freaks like me can be more irritating than untidy beings - I often annoy the crap out of myself with my habitual need to put things away, only to find I need the item again a minute later. I did hope she'd bought her sense of humour along with her.

We had a ball. Laughed ourselves silly - unfortunately usually at other people's expense. We were the odd ones on board, being Australian . Well actually Angie is very English, but lives in Australia so we include her as one of us. The 3000 odd passengers were predominantly American - it was an American cruise-ship after-all. We were delighted to find little towel animals in our cabin each night, with chocolate squares left for us. We were easy pleased.

We quickly developed a regular routine of me arising and doing my yoga in a little area tucked away from Angie's bed, so as not to disturb her with my pranayama and alternate nostril breathing, while she slept till eight every morning! Then me disappearing for a brisk walk up on the top deck while she fiddled and diddled and got herself ready for the day. Then finally being ready to go to breakfast. We lasted two days at the buffet breakfast before we could take no more of watching people piling their plates so high that food was falling off the sides, and returning for second and third helpings. These were people who clearly should not have been going for second and third helpings! That old mentality of "I've paid for this so I'm gonna stuff myself full" was working on overload. Day three and beyond found us in the formal restaurant for a more civilized breakfast. Day three was also the day we discovered the ice cream machines on the pool deck. Who's calling the kettle black now?

Our first evening meal was very entertaining. Disorganised chaos would be a better way to describe it. But it did improve as the nights went on. We were placed on a table for ten, two of whom never showed up for the entire cruise. We can only assume they chose the buffet option for their evening meals. We were glad we never had the pleasure actually. The other three couples were a mixed bunch - couple one were painfully shy and dreary and only spoke when spoken to. Couple two were not so shy but still dreary and even though they did speak, they didn't actually have anything to say. The third couple were delightful, he Romanian and very gregarious and opinionated, and she Dutch and adoring of her husband. They were very animated and we had some interesting discussions. These were our table mates for the duration of the cruise - I think they finally warmed to us by the end. Or were just bemused by us. We did provide a few laughs for them. Especially when we both flirted pathetically with our Croatian waiter. Both competing for the same prize. That's never good.

Our days at sea were spent exploring the ship and its various activities. Angie attended an 'art appreciation' class while I checked out the 'Abba dance' class - yes there really is such a thing. We would then rejoin to partake in judging the 'hairy chest' competition - I'm joking, we didn't judge it, we couldn't even bring ourselves to watch it. You could say the daytime activities were not all that appealing to us. We did develop a routine (one of many by this stage) of having an afternoon nap followed by a gin and tonic in our cabin before preparing for the evening meal. The first formal night was an eye opener. One woman's interpretation of formal was wearing thongs (flip-flops to you non Aussies) adorned with fur and sparkles. Very glamorous indeed.

Most of our amusement though came from the questions we were asked about Australia. These three were asked of me while I waited in a queue to speak to the purser:

1) So how are you enjoying joining the Euro currency in Australia?

I'd only been gone a week, when did that happen?

2) So where about's in Europe *is* Australia?

Oh, its tiny really. It's wedged in between Belgium and Luxemburg, it's so small.

3) My personal favourite –

Where exactly *is* Australia?

My actual answer to this lady :

"Well, you know Indonesia?" (clearly not judging from the blank look on her face)

"Okay, you know where China is?"

Yes, I'm on a winner!

"Well, we're south of there"!!!

Do these people use different world maps to us? Just what is in that huge space south of the equator if we're not on their map?

What was more frightening from this revelation was 'how did this woman manage to get from her home country to Rome to board this ship?' Clearly someone held her hand every step of the way.

And yet another jaw-dropping observation from a cute little reggae man who ran the disco - "I can't wait to get to Australia. I'm gonna get me one of your spider monkey's for a pet". Spider monkeys? I think he had his continents confused. Or did he mean possums? In which case you wouldn't want one for a pet.

By the third day at sea, we'd become bored with the ship's daytime activities. We were back in our cabin, boredom clearly set in.

"Can I borrow your nail scissors?" I asked Angie, quite dejectedly.

"Oh come on Judi, pull yourself together. It's not worth slitting your wrists over" replied Angie, "think of all that mess I'll have to clean up."

I nearly wet myself laughing. Actually no, I think I did.

"Bury me at sea" I managed to blurt out in between fits of laughter "they'll never find Australia to send my body home!"

Our cute Croatian waiter who we'd both been competing for, invited us to a private audience with him to listen to his piano playing. He actually wrote out a personal invitation to each of us - how sweet. Problem was, the only time he could get access to the piano in the piano bar was three in the morning! So we set our alarm to wake us up in time (how sad is that - we couldn't last the distance till then) and set off in expectation of what I'm not sure of. Our 'personal' invitations had been extended to five or six other ladies, all much younger than us! We felt cheated! We actually thought one of us was in with a chance! But he *was* a beautiful pianist. I'm sure he had a beautiful penis too.

Port days became tedious too believe it or not. The ship had docked in Cannes, offshore. The only port that you had to catch a tender to shore. It was overcast and cold. We lay on our beds after breakfast.

"Do we really have to go ashore today?" I asked Angie.

"Yes, I know how you feel, it's all become a bit ho-hum hasn't it?"

Another bout of hysterics as we realized the implication of what we had just said.

"Oh god, we are terrible aren't we? There are people back home in their dreary everyday lives with their dreary wives and husbands who'd give their eye teeth to be where we are right now" I laughed " and here we are debating whether we can be bothered exploring the French Riviera for the day!" We forced ourselves to go in the end.

We were spoilt weren't we? Trouble was, we'd both been to every place on this cruise, bar Dubrovnic. We were both quite well travelled. And becoming travel snobs.

The cruise came to an end, we'd had a great laugh. I didn't find any cute cabin boys to play up with and we headed off to Calpe.

I stayed with Angie in her flat the first two nights as George wasn't arriving till the Monday. We were only going to have five days together.

I checked into the hotel I'd stayed in previously on the Monday morning. I'd requested a room with a sea-view, the girl had remembered me from that previous visit, so upgraded me to their honeymoon suite. She was quite taken with my story about George and how we hadn't seen each other for three months.

Chapter 7

Tablecloth, Anyone?

I waited around excitedly for George to arrive. I had champagne on ice ready in the room. He called to say he was just leaving the airport and would be half an hour.

He called again five minutes later to say he was in the foyer and would I like to come down to greet him. Up to his old tricks again. Just as well I was ready!

It was wonderful seeing him again. We hugged and kissed for ages right there in the hotel lobby. We sat and chatted over a drink. One of George's first things he said to me was "we need to sort out what we want to do, because I want you over here with me. I want to spend the rest of my life with you". We headed up to our room.

I knew we wouldn't surface for a few hours, and so did my friend at reception.

Our days started with lazy breakfasts and a walk along the promenade. Lazing on the beach and many swims in the sea followed. We both loved swimming and behaved like kids again, splashing and pulling each other under water, kissing and cuddling, fondling and the obligatory pulling down each others swimmers. I'd forgotten what such a simple pleasure all this was, it had been a lifetime since I'd behaved like this.

George is an avid newspaper reader and loves crosswords, so that's what he did while I sunbathed on the sand. Still topless of course. I loved the liberating feeling, especially swimming topless. George enjoyed it too, I have to add. We were very relaxed and comfortable in each other's company.

Each night we would walk arm in arm along the promenade and choose a restaurant for dinner. It was usually on the seafront, the views were too good to pass up. These restaurants were in the habit of setting up tables out front offering free glasses of sangria to lure you in. George was such a softie, he always got taken in by that. We were seated at one of these restaurants one night when this gentleman proceeded to show me tablecloths of all shapes and sizes. In my innocence I thought he was the restaurant owner wanting my opinion on new napery for the tables. He must have opened out twenty of these garish cloths before the penny dropped. George of course was enjoying every moment of this, not offering me any hint of what it was about.

Finally he couldn't contain himself anymore and put the poor man out of his misery, dismissing him with a feeble explanation of "she's from Australia you know, she has no clue what you're on about". As if being Australian pardoned me from my stupidity, like saying "she has Alzheimer's you know. You'll have to excuse her". Mind you, I was to learn that it could be a very handy excuse to use in my varied travels.

How was I to know he was trying to sell me a tablecloth? Who'd of thought that while you're enjoying a dinner on holidays, someone would be peddling napery to you? And why, more's the point? We fell about laughing. Poor man, he had to fold all his cloths back up again and hadn't made a penny!

Of course, these pedlars were everywhere along the beachfront. Usually African immigrants, selling handbags and jewellery but mostly sunglasses and watches - to people who clearly were already wearing sunglasses and watches. I did admire their tenacity.

This was a curious phenomenon to me, we don't have this kind of practice in Australia. The most you might find is an occasional ice cream/drinks barrow man making his way around the bathers. Anything more than that would probably incite a riot over our invasion of privacy.

We chose a restaurant off the main promenade one night that had a lovely garden area at the front. There was only one other couple seated. The waitress bought our menus to us with the following warning:
"I must tell you that your order could take an hour or longer to arrive."

"If you don't wish to wait that long, we understand."

"'ow long?" George exclaimed.

She went on to tell us that all the staff had left, there was just her and her husband to do everything, and they were trying to sell the restaurant if we were interested.

Wow, no wonder the place was packed! This greeting from the maitre d' would really pull in the punters wouldn't it? We were so taken back with her desperate honesty that we couldn't bear to leave. So we ordered our meals and hoped for the best. We spent the next hour drinking their wine (was this story just a ploy I wondered, to ply you full of alcohol first so you wouldn't care how bad the food was?) George kept us all (the other two diners as well) amused with his joke telling and antics. We were all having such a raucous time that it actually attracted more diners into the restaurant! Oh dear, how were the owners going to cope? Should we offer to help out with the cooking we wondered? Or the washing up?

Our food eventually arrived and it was actually very nice. An odd combination though. I had ordered pork chops which came with not only vegetables but a fruit selection on the side of the plate. Main course and dessert all in one - the chef obviously thought it would save more waiting. By this time we were in that silly mood that hits after copious amounts of wine and laughter. We started planning our own restaurant, coming up with the most absurd combinations of food to serve - ice cream drizzled with balsamic vinegar, lettuce soup, that kind of thing. George would be the maitre d', pulling them in off the street. Quite literally - we decided that the owner's sympathy tactic could work a treat. He would then pass among the diners helping himself to their food as he chatted to them - could you imagine the reaction?

We laughed and giggled the night away. The chef and his wife eventually pulled up a chair each and joined us, opened a new bottle of wine on the house and declared the night had been the best in ages. They were a delightful couple, he was Dutch and she from Estonia, and they were really doing it tough. They were losing money hand over fist and were considering just shutting the doors on the place. Hmm, our zany restaurant idea could be a reality, we mused together. All in all, we spent over four hours in the place.

We stumbled across (again, quite literally - we had a huge amount of wine already under our belts) a fantastic bar in one of the streets running off the dry river bed that runs into the sea. Called Sinatra's, complete with a great neon sign of the man himself tipping his hat. The owner - another Dutch man - was a terrific bloke. This bar went on to become our signature bar, our hang out. Gary (not very Dutch I thought) made the best Pina Colada's we'd both ever tasted.

Better than that though, was his amazing computer system that could pull up any song you requested, from anywhere in the world. Of course, this encouraged a betting competition with him that we never won. I know what you're thinking, you loyal Australians who stand to attention, swell with pride and sing the house down every time you hear our adopted anthem played in the pubs! Yes, of course I asked if he could find Jimmy Barnes singing Kay San! And blow me down, he did! I was in love with him!

Our third night was spent in Benidorm, the nightlife capital of mainland Spain. More about Benidorm later. We caught a cab, it cost around fifty euros - this was going to be an expensive night. George had been there before, first some twenty five odd years ago on his honeymoon, and again on a lad's week away. So he knew what to expect. We had an enjoyable messy meal in Tony Roma's, a steak and rib restaurant known the world over.

We then began our bar hopping evening. Entertainment was on tap. Every cabaret bar offered a string of entertainment, all in one hour stints, that continued until well after two in the morning. And, incredibly nowhere was there a cover charge. Absolutely free, just the cost of your drinks. And they were the cheapest I'd seen anywhere.

Where would we start? The comedians of course. Now anyone that's ever been to a comedy night will know that you find a seat in an inconspicuous area towards the back of the room to avoid being targeted by the man at centre stage. Not when you're with George I'm afraid! No, we sat dead centre right in front of the microphone! Oh god, what was I in for? The most laughs I've ever had as it turned out! George was of course, a great heckler who knew when to apply it and when to stop. The comedians loved it, the banter between them was magical. I got picked on, for being Australian. Some of the acts we saw were top class, and we were to become repeat customers. Interspersed with the comedy acts we took in a couple of tribute acts, which were also fantastic. Who were these people that performed in this town? Complete unknowns in their home country, but hugely popular here.

Around one in the morning George started seeking out the venue for the town's most famous act, which he first saw those twenty five odd years ago. She was still performing! This lady was now well into her sixties, still doing the same magic act and I was gobsmacked! Too incredibly clever and talented to be offensive, shall I just say that she left nothing to the imagination as items appeared from certain parts of her anatomy that I never realised had so many uses!

We found ourselves in a nightclub after that. A great atmosphere with incredible music that although wasn't my taste, was mesmerising to listen to. George arrived back to me with another drink for us. His mood had reduced to quite a sombre one out of the blue. As I looked at him wondering what was going on in his head, he blurted out "you won't come over here to live with me, will you? You won't leave your kids and job to be with me?"

Where did that come from? He looked absolutely shattered, like his world had fallen in.

"Why are you saying this stuff?" I asked.

"Why are you thinking that? We haven't even talked about it", I continued. I was dumbfounded. How had he concluded this without us even having discussed anything.

"I just know you won't. I can tell" he stammered dejectedly.

"That's not fair for you to make that assumption. You haven't even asked me" I retorted. I was getting really frustrated by now.

"I want you here with me, I want to spend the rest of my life with you, but I know you won't leave what you've got behind to be with me" he continued. Now he was just talking in circles.

I kissed him and hugged him. I told him I would give up everything to be with him, that I loved him more than I ever felt possible. But he hadn't asked me to move over to be with him, so how could I know that's what he wanted.

"You've never asked me, so how can I answer you?" I continued.

With that he asked me to marry him.

Of course I said yes. I'd been hoping for this day to come.

We headed down to the beach with the intention of making love again. It wasn't possible though as it was very open and very well lit with security patrols everywhere.

I desperately needed to pee, so I squatted in the sand behind the pile of sunbeds while George kept a look out. The things you lower yourself to when you're drunk.

I think we eventually arrived back at our hotel around six in the morning. We slept most of the day. Nothing more was said of our conversation the night before until later that night. We had returned to Sinatra's bar for more alcohol, our bodies were in withdrawal phase by this stage of the holiday.

"About last night", I started. "did you mean what you said? What you asked me?"

"I absolutely did. Of course I meant it. Why wouldn't I" he answered.

"You were very drunk. I'd like to hear it again with you sober. So I know you mean it." This wasn't unreasonable of me to ask was it?

With that he got down on bended knee, took my hand and proposed to me. Properly. In front of half a dozen people in the bar. And sober.

"Judi, I think you're the most gorgeous, lovely, funny, caring, sexy woman I've ever known and I want to spend the rest of my life with you. I love you with all my heart. Will you marry me?"

You could have heard a pin drop. Everyone was holding their breath, even the old drunk on the stool in the corner who'd been talking to himself.

"Of course I will, you gorgeous man. I thought you'd never ask" was my reply.

Great cheers erupted, hugs all round. We bought a round of drinks. Every one else bought us a round of drinks. Gary played my song for me. It was a wonderful night. We were legless by the time we left. But we were sober when George proposed to me this time. That's all that mattered.

One more day together. We talked about how we were going to do this - this getting married thing. He had to get a divorce first. Not as easy as it sounds. I assumed that because he got married in Australia, he could get divorced under our law and just need to be separated for a year. Not so, they no longer lived in Australia so had to divorce under English law. They aren't so quick at handing out divorces there.

Not to worry, there was no rush. We would be happy to live together until then.

We made a plan - I would return home, sell my townhouse that I lived in but keep his old house - my investment home. I would get as many sales as I could under way to pay off my debts and so have enough money to get by on from the profits of my townhouse. Maybe use it to buy something in Spain or England. Wherever we decided to settle. Spain was the more favourable option to both of us. George was uncomfortable with the suggestion of using my money to buy something. He would have to contribute his own share, he stated. Whatever, I wasn't bothered by that kind of thing. We decided on a suitable time for this to happen and agreed that we would be together again six months from now.

I was on cloud nine. So was George. We laughed, we swam, we did crosswords together (he saved some for me - this proved he loved me!), we made love in the afternoon. We dined in the lovely German restaurant I had discovered on my previous visit. My mixed grill was served in a frying pan! How quirky. Less washing up, I guessed. The most enormous meal, I barely made a dent in it. If we'd known we would have shared one dish. I broke the back of my chair when I leant on it to get up. The head chef yelled abuse at his cooks the entire time - it was an open kitchen. We weren't game to point out that George's steak was a little over done! Another amusing night dining out in Calpe. Honestly, I've never had a dull evening in a restaurant there. A final stop off in Sinatra's. Gary made our favourite cocktails again for us. He wished us well. We said he was coming to the wedding, as long as he bought his computer. I loved this town and couldn't wait to come back again.

We parted at Alicante airport. It was very tearful. I felt like I was going to throw up. This was the hardest goodbye ever. I cried the entire one hour flight to Paris. The poor man sitting next to me, it made him very uncomfortable. I told him why I was crying. He was very happy for me. Well he would be, he was French. Romantics, all of them.

Chapter 8

Sister Squabbles

I had time to pull myself together and reflect on the events of the past week. My daughters weren't arriving till the following morning, so I had a night to myself in Paris. Oh how I wished George was with me now. How romantic to be in Paris with the man you love. The reality was though, that I would have to drug George and smuggle him blindfolded onto a plane bound for Paris - or anywhere in France for that matter. He had an unhealthy despise of all things French. These English, will they ever forgive and forget?

My girls arrived safely and we spent two more nights in Paris. My youngest had never been here or anywhere in Europe so this was to be a memorable trip for her. It certainly was, as you'll see later. Our hotel was wonderful, in the Latin Quarter right amongst the hustle and bustle of the busy little restaurant streets and a block away from the River Seine. Sadly, I couldn't share my elation with them. Neither of them approved of my relationship with this married man who just up and left me three months previously. It was wrong on every level according to them.

To me it was a fairytale. I was in love with a gorgeous funny man who wanted to spend his life with me in some faraway place. At my age true love doesn't happen all that often. Sometimes never. So I wasn't bothered with the moral details of the story.

"I feel like I'm hiding some huge secret from my girls, and I am. I feel so bad, but I can't tell them. They'd be mortified" I said in my text to George. He kind of understood - thought they were just frightened of losing their mother to him. He didn't know they had a real issue with him personally, and I wasn't about to tell him. I loved him, they didn't.

Our driving tour of Europe started off well. I did all the driving though, so I didn't really take in the scenery. It was very tiring, I would sometimes drive for six or seven hours to get to our next destination. Not exactly fun for me.

"If I ever suggest a driving tour for our honeymoon, you have my permission to shoot me" I messaged to George.

"I'll keep that in mind" he replied. "Safe driving, and not too many arguments I hope" he added.

I wished he hadn't said that. About the arguments I mean.

By day seven of our trip, my girls had a huge row over something trivial I'm sure (one wearing the other's top or some such) and spent the next three days not talking to each other. It was most uncomfortable. They were like little kids again, passing messages to me to relay to each other. One would wait in the car while the other ate and vice versa.

Oh please! Do I need this! They're grown women for god's sake. Where was George when I needed him?

They eventually started talking again, but not before my patience had worn thin with the whole touring thing. This was not my idea of a holiday, driving all day and being too tired at the end of the day to do anything more than eat and go to bed. What a contrast from the previous week! Even though the girls were fine again, they both decided they'd had enough and that they would bring their departure day forward by two days. *They* were able to pick up their flight in Frankfurt, Germany instead of departing from Paris, and they could catch a flight that night if they could get to the airport in time.

Where were we you ask? Just heading into the Italian alps! We'd just left our hotel in northern Italy after breakfast, so on their whim, I had to drive across the Alps and up to Frankfurt by nightfall. Fortunately, both were good at reading maps and navigating so we were able to plan out the easiest route to take. As always, things look so easy on a map. What they don't show is the narrow winding roads just wide enough for one car to pass, the steep drops down the mountain on the side of the road, roadblocks, roadworks, etc, etc.

For a good part of these steep windy roads, I never made it out of first gear. I was fearful of burning the clutch out, or the brakes on the downhill run. At the very crest of the mountain range, we drove through an electrical storm - that was fun.

There were some enjoyable moments though. The scenery was spectacular and we had a beautiful lunch at a little Italian restaurant on top of one of the mountains. And we did drive through some gorgeous quaint little villages that we would never have seen otherwise. We passed through the border into Austria and back out again. Finally we were on an autobahn and I was able to make up time. Driving at 160 kph was exhilarating to me. The roads are fantastic in Germany and are very safe. Even at those speeds I was still being overtaken!

By some way of a miracle we made it in time to Frankfurt airport. I had to take special note of where I parked the car, or I might never find it again. We said our goodbyes and they were on their way home. I, on the other hand was left stranded in a busy airport facing the daunting task of finding my way out of there and onto a road heading to France at 11 o'clock at night.

My flight could not be changed - because of the special price I had got it for or some such nonsense. So I had to hang around another two days - alone again. By the grace of my guardian angels who travel with me, I managed to recognise a few signs heading out of the airport that lead me directly onto the road I needed to be on. All signs in Germany are, astoundingly, in German! My entire grasp of the German language equates to a few swear words I learnt from my ex husband and his family. You could say my Spanish and German could do with some improvement. A lot of good that revelation was to me at this moment.

I stopped somewhere along the way to check my map, the last thing I needed was to take a wrong turn. I had to make my way to Strasbourg just over the border in France to drop off the hire car. They were going to charge me some exorbitant price for a drop off in another country, so that was my reason for heading back into France.

I stopped at every service station along the highway trying to find a room for the night. I had been driving for about fourteen hours non stop and I was exhausted. I needed to sleep. Just as I was seriously considering just curling up in the back seat of the car in the parking lot and risking my life for the chance of a sleep, I made one last enquiry at the next service station. This kind lady made a phone call to the next travel centre along the way, and they had a room available for me. These travel centres have motels attached to them, wonderful for the business man who spends his days on the road. Or for clandestine liaisons.

I was so grateful to her for her help and finally flopped into a clean bed at somewhere near one in the morning. I didn't care what the cost was, in fact I don't think I even asked until check out, I just needed to sleep.

The next two days dragged by. I managed to find the drop off point for the car and made my way by train back to Frankfurt. I almost got arrested by the German rail police for not having a ticket. I had printed out a receipt but couldn't work out how to get the actual ticket from the machine, (again it was in German!) so just boarded the train thinking that would be okay. The train system in Germany is policed by descendants of the Gestapo it would appear. After much eyelid batting and pleading ignorance (I was Australian you know), I managed to sweet talk my way out of a fine. Not before I was given a private lesson on how to use their ticket machines!

Checked into a cheap hotel somewhere near the city - in quite a rough area as it turned out - and tried to fill in the next two days. I was all travelled out. Frankfurt isn't the most touristy place to occupy your time, it's a lovely city but unless you're into shopping there's not much else on offer. Not to someone who's tired and over travelling anyway.

I whiled away the hours reading a book down by the river near my hotel. Until the last afternoon, where I turned up a little street and found the most authentically German square that I could have been exploring had I known it was there. Complete with archway entrance and cobbled lanes, it was delightful. I had dinner there and sampled some German beer and of course apple strudel.

Fortunately I had my messages to and from George to keep me company. I kept him updated on my whereabouts. He was genuinely worried that I was alone in Frankfurt. He didn't know that I was actually quite used to travelling alone and it didn't particularly bother me. Like so many others, he couldn't grasp the concept of a woman travelling on her own and actually enjoying it. I on the other hand, feel that sometimes the advantages outweigh the disadvantages.

Finally it was time for me to fly home. I was glad. I had plans to put in place. Houses to sell, money to earn, people to see. I couldn't wait to land.

Chapter 9

High's and Lo's

Back home to reality. My business needed sorting, contracts needed following up. I had been running my own business from home for twelve months now. The new office I had managed turned out to be a bit of a sham, the owner turning quite nasty over some things that Angie was eluding to as a means of acquiring some of the money she had previously invested with him. Although it wasn't directed at me, I knew it was time to bail, before I did get dragged into it. So with no prospects of where to go, and quite frankly no office I wanted to go to, I set up my own business from my home. My previous clients were very supportive of me and I had no trouble getting it under way.

It never ceases to amaze me what one can achieve when their hand is forced. Here I was jobless with no income and fed up with being taken advantage of. So within half an hour of signing myself off that last managerial position, I had a business name registered, a new logo designed and business cards and stationery ordered at the printers. It cost me less than five hundred dollars.

Should have done it sooner, I told myself on a number of occasions. For it was within that first twelve months that I had earnt enough money for those two overseas trips, and bought an investment property. Not that there weren't lean times too - there were to be many - but I was used to the roller-coaster world of making a living from selling real estate.

Nicole, my eldest daughter had decided to join me in my business just prior to that first trip to visit my friend in Italy and then Spain. Talk about being thrown in at the deep end! Within less than a month she was taking care of business while I was off sunning myself in Spain. Did a damn fine job of it too. She was a natural, I could see it already.

So I had no hesitation in taking that second trip, knowing she was more than capable of looking after things in my absence. Of course, the two weeks that she joined me with her sister in France the business just had to go into a holding pattern. Not much was happening at that time, so there really was no problem.

But now I really needed to earn some serious money. Not just to make up for lost time, but I now had something more exciting to plan for. I was getting married and going to live in Spain next year! So with head down and tail up I set to adding more listings to my stock and marketing them. It was hard work but I thrived. I always work better when I'm really busy, it motivates me.

Communications with George kept me going. The texting continued, lots of sweet messages late at night and plenty of funny ones too. I was blooming. My friend's could see it. I wear my heart on my sleeve and everyone could see how happy I was. The act of being in love and knowing that that person loves you back is euphoric. Happiness makes me happy. And content. I floated along in my new state of being.

I bumped into Tommy one day at the shopping centre. George's old friend who was going through the marriage break-up. I told him I'd just got back from spending five days with George and of course shared my exciting news with him. He was really happy for me, although a bit surprised. He confided in me that he had always questioned why George married his second wife, he had admitted to not loving her even a week before their wedding. Went ahead with it anyway.

As the weeks wore on, the texts and emails slowed down. That's okay, I thought. Its to be expected. He's probably just busy getting back into work as I am. He'd already admitted he's not very good at keeping in touch when he's busy. So I just let it go. A few more weeks went by. The contact had stopped.

I ran into Tommy again. I got all teary with him and he said he'd try and contact George to find out what was going on. I gave him my number. He called the next day and arranged to meet me for a drink. What he had to say to me struck right through the heart.

He'd asked George straight out if it was true that he'd asked me to marry him.

"I was pissed" was George's reply. "I'm not going to marry her."

I was gutted. Tommy was gutted at seeing my reaction. He gave me a few home truth's about George to try and soften the blow. It didn't. He hugged me and said he was truly sorry but I needed to know what he'd said. I thanked him for his honesty and left.

My world fell apart. I couldn't function. I felt so alone. I remember one night breaking down completely in my garden. I just sobbed and sobbed. I sat on the damp grass under the moonlight pulling weeds out of the garden and weeping. I cried myself to exhaustion. I wanted to sleep more than anything. Sleep the pain away. I took a couple of strong sleeping tablets. Then regretted it. My body wasn't used to drugs. So I rang Angie and told her what I'd done and would she check on me in the morning? I knew it wouldn't kill me, but may have doped me out for longer than it should have.

I withdrew for about a week. My business suffered. I didn't want to think about anything, just sleep it off. Didn't want to see my friends, how could I face them? Didn't talk about it to anyone but Angie, and certainly not my daughters. They knew what had happened, you only had to look at me to know. They discreetly said nothing.

Somewhere during that week I found the strength to email George. The first was short and blunt. Something about him not having the courage to tell me himself, that he figured I'd finally get the hint by his ignoring me. More about how his poor mate had to do his dirty work for him. Then another calmer one, asking him what went wrong? Why couldn't he have just told me he'd changed his mind? Yes he might have been pissed that first night, but certainly wasn't the second time he asked me to marry him. What about the plans we made? He wasn't drunk then. What cruel games you're playing, I said.

I heard nothing for at least a month. I pulled myself together and got on with life. A couple of trips to the beach and long lone walks along the sand are my salvation. Something about that clean salt air clears my head. My friends always know where to look when I need time out to contemplate. And they graciously let me have that time to myself.

Just before Christmas he contacted me. He still wanted me. He was sorry about what had happened, he had just freaked out a bit. I didn't know how I felt. My brain was warning me to be cautious but my heart just wanted to jump right back in. My heart won. I did jump back in. The text messages flowed freely again. We never rang each other, which was curious I know. Many people thought he was too tight to spend the money on a phone call and I can understand their thinking. He wasn't tight with money at all, but only I knew that. I always had a hard time understanding him on the phone and we tended to talk over the top of each other, so we both just found texting easier.

Boxing day I sent a message saying "Please call me, after much soul searching I've made a moment-ous decision today I want to share with you."

The following morning my phone rang. His number appeared on my screen.

"Judi, this is Jane. George's wife. Why are you sending these text messages to him? About soul searching and decisions? What is going on?"

I was dumbfounded. I stumbled through a few words of reply and then the phone cut out thankfully. His battery must have died right at the appropriate moment. My guardian angels once more looking out for me.

Oh god. Here I go again. This time I didn't fall apart. I got angry. What kind of double life was this man living? I sent an email - I didn't dare message his phone. Although she deserved to know, I thought.

"My momentous decision I was so excited to tell you about was that I had set a date - Sunday 1st April - to move over to Spain to live with you...................."

Well, that wasn't going to happen now, was it? The next day, another email to this cad.

"I wish I had someone to hold me right now. I've never felt more alone in my life. Or betrayed."

When I started thinking back to our trip to Calpe some three months earlier, it occurred to me that he never actually admitted that he had left Jane. I never thought to ask. I just assumed he had. My stupidity. My father always taught me never to assume, I should have listened to him.

Finally an email the next day. He had left his phone on her dining table. She read all the texts I'd sent him over the last six months. He didn't care, he wanted a divorce. She was being a real pain. He went on to say how things are really complicated, he's got job offers in three different countries, doesn't know what he's doing, blah, blah, blah.

I didn't know if I had the energy for him any more. He ran so hot and cold. What was it that kept drawing me back to him? I wish I knew. I just kept going back for more. We spoke on the phone that night. I still didn't know where I stood after the conversation. Things just chugged along for the next few weeks.

My townhouse had been on the market since before Christmas. I had decided even after the heartbreak with George that I couldn't afford to keep it anymore and I'd be better off renting and keeping the investment property for a while. The market had slowed right down and my finances were tight again. I'd had very little in the way of sales and at this point couldn't even sell my own place.

After another month of nothing definite from George, I sent him a long email telling him I didn't know if I could continue like this. Could he just let me know if there was any hope of us being together? If not, I'll move on and get on with my life. But this uncertainty was wearing me down. I always felt better when I'd written my thoughts down.

He replied with a rather lengthy email which was unusual. Yes, he did love me with all his heart, I was the most (here was about ten adjectives describing what he thought of me) woman he'd ever known, and prattled on about being old fashioned and being the provider, always the bread winner and he felt he couldn't be that with me. What I read between the lines was that he felt inferior to me, was threatened by the fact that I had more than him financially and he didn't know how to deal with it.

So that was what this was about? Pride? Damn, stupid man! God, why do we bother with them? I'd been put on an emotional roller coaster because of his damn English pride. Get a grip, I wanted to tell him.

Instead, in my usual diplomatic way I painstakingly explained to him how none of his concerns mattered to me. I'm not materialistic in any way, not worried who's got what financially and all I really wanted was to be with him somewhere - anywhere. Couldn't he understand that? Obviously not. He drifted away from me again.

After a week or two I sent him a clever (I thought) ditty I'd composed about us, hoping it would appeal to his comedic side:

Ode to George

There once was a fella from Yorkshire
Who kept teasing a lady from Oz
He kept saying he'd call her and send presents for her
But he never - cos that's how he woz

So she waited with all of her patience
For him to decide to come good
But her friends, well they were all cynics
Just kept saying that he never would

"Don't you know that all men are bastards?"
Like a chorus together they clucked
When will you finally realise
And tell him to go and get fucked

But this lady from Oz couldn't do it
For she truly wanted to believe
That her George, well he was just different
So she'd forever give him a reprieve!

To be continued.........................

"Feel free to complete it" I added.

Nothing. No response.

I couldn't take anymore. I sent a really long email a few weeks later:

"Hi.

I'm sorry but I can't do this any more. I can't put my life on hold waiting to see if you're ever gonna want me. It hurts being ignored, hearing you say you're gonna do something then never hearing from you. I adore you being the funny man, but there are some things in life that should be taken seriously, even by you. As the months have dragged on, I've seen a side of you I didn't know existed. And it's knocked me for six. A side that doesn't care for or about anyone, especially me. You've become so self-absorbed in your own life, you don't realize (or care) what hurt you're causing to others.

I've laughed off & tried to understand your need to sort yourself out since you left Australia, I understand that you're enjoying the freedom you have, but I've finally come to realize that I'm just hanging on to a fantasy and so are you.

This nonsense about you needing to be the bread-winner is just a copout. This is the 21st century, not the dark ages. I've been on my own for nearly 8 years,

85

what would you expect me to do? I don't like to "put on" anyone either - if I did I would have found some rich guy ages ago & sponged off him. But instead I got off my arse & got myself into a job where I could actually earn some decent money to make a nice life for myself, with nobody's help. I shouldn't have to apologise for my achievements, I should be proud of them.

What hurts me George is that the very things about me that you were attracted to in the beginning are now the things that have driven you away - that I'm strong, confidant, independant, self-sufficient, can make my own decisions & don't need anyone to support me - have now become qualities that you can't deal with. I wish you could just be proud of me for them, not scared because of them.

You know sometimes I get tired of being the strong one & just wish there was someone who'd put their arms around me & tell me I don't have to be those things anymore, and I so wanted you to be that person. But you won't do that, will you?

We've known each other two years now & I think I've been very patient. I've accepted being the "other" woman & not put any demands on you. But I need more than that now. I want & need someone who not only loves me & misses me as you say you do, but **wants** me too. Wants to see me, can't wait to see me, wants to talk to me, email me, text me.

I need someone who is proud to tell the world about me, show me off to their family & friends. Not keep me a deep dark secret like they're ashamed of me. I don't want to be just an afterthought. I deserve better than that, I think. And I thought I was worth a plane ticket to see, or at the very least the cost of a phone call.

You keep telling me of things you're "gonna" do - you ask for my address & I check my mailbox for a month & nothing comes, you ask for it again & again nothing comes, you ask for my phone number cos you're gonna call me, & nothing. No gift, no flowers, not even a card. You don't even keep my card in your wallet now - what does that tell me?

And worst of all, you ask me to marry you -twice- & change your mind. These are cruel games you're playing. I never believed you'd be capable of this, I thought you were my perfect man. I guess my ex was right, that you men are all the same, telling us what we want to hear just to string us along.

Well as I said, I can't do this anymore. I believe I'm worth more. And I thought that you thought I was worth more. I'm really sad about this, you know that. But I have to let you go. We joked in Calpe about what our first fight would be like - we're never gonna know are we? And that's a shame, cause making up would have been wonderful.

I'll always love you - but you know that too.

I finished the ditty........

But this lady from Oz couldn't do it
For she truly wanted to believe
That her George, well he was just different
So she'd forever give him a reprieve!

Wouldn't you know it - he just ignored her
So that told her what she needed to know
That he really didn't care for or want her
So with sadness she did let him go

The End

Chapter 10

Aunty Joyce

I did let him go. Or so I thought. I never stopped thinking about him. I'd wake up thinking of him, I'd go to sleep thinking of him. But I didn't contact him. I was determined to be strong. Work began to pick up. I took my house off the market, it wasn't meant to sell obviously. I am a firm believer in things happening for a reason. It wasn't the right time for me to be out of a home. I needed the stability around me.

Two months went by. Out of the blue I received an email from him with one of those lovely power point shows attached - a paradox of life. It was lovely. He hadn't written anything, just put in the subject line "I will always love you. I can't ever forget you."

"What is this supposed to mean, I don't get it" I replied.

Another two weeks. Another lovely power point show email. This one titled "Things Aren't Always What They Seem".

"Very sweet. I know, things aren't always what they seem. If only I could work out what they are meant to be" was my brief reply.

Came the reply:

"Hope your well and still as sexy. Keep in touch gorgeous, love you forever. George the nugget xxxxxxxxxxxxxxxxxxxxxxxxxxxxxxxxxxxxxxxxxxxxxxxxx xxxx"

I'd had a phone call from an insurance company urgently looking for him. They had tracked me down as the new owner of his house. I told them nothing, but felt I should let him know in case it was really important. So I emailed very briefly to tell him.

He did reply with an update about what he was up to. Still declared his love for me but at least this time he was honest enough to tell me he didn't really know what he wanted and would stay put in this new job for a while till he worked out what it was he did want. He was travelling all over Europe con-structing sets for an exhibition company he'd worked for a few times before.

I had been going through a fairly traumatic time myself so gave him an update about it. One of my sisters had just had a major heart operation and wasn't fairing very well. She had been in intensive care on life support since the operation, we were now into her third week and still had no indication as to whether she would pull through. I had been to the hospital every day with her twin sister to visit her and sit by her, and I was pretty stressed and tired. My blood pressure had shot through the roof so had to abandon the gym for a bit in case I blew a fuse.

Enough time had gone by that I was able to send this update without any expectation of what might be. I reflected on what a great time we'd had and wished him well.

My sister finally came off life support and was able to breathe on her own. She'd passed the worst of it. We were all so relieved. My two aunt's from Sydney had called every other day, so it was with great relief I was able to phone them both a week later to tell them we could finally take her home. It was lovely to speak to them with some positive news for a change. It had been a really worrying time for all of us.

The following morning I drove my daughter and her partner to the airport, they were off to Port Douglas for a few days. My sister (the one just home from hospital) had called while I was driving and spoke to Nicole. Asked her to get me to call in to their home on the way back. Couldn't it wait till tomorrow, I asked? I had a lot of work to catch up on.

"No", Nicole replied, "it will only take you a minute to drop in."

"Okay then, but I can't stay". I thought that maybe my sister had a present for me or something for driving up to the hospital every day for a month.

I arrived at my sisters' house and my younger daughter had just pulled up as well. Odd, I thought, why would she be visiting them this morning?
Michelle came over to me as I got out of the car.

"Aunty Joyce died last night."

This had a devastating effect on me. I just couldn't believe it. She was my rock. I thought she'd always be in my life.

"She was supposed to live forever" I sobbed to my sisters. Not my gorgeous Aunty Joyce, this just isn't happening.

She had an abdominal aneurism that burst with no warning. She hadn't been to a doctor in years she was so healthy. My poor uncle had to be questioned by police because she had no recent medical records. They had to rule out foul play, they said.

She was 83, but as I say, as healthy as an ox. The funniest lady I ever knew. She was closer to me than my own mother had been when she was alive. The matriach of our family, she kept us all together. I loved her humour, we adored each other. I couldn't imagine my life without her in it.

Uncle Brian and their only son were completely devastated. They too thought she'd be around for many more years. Her mother lived to ninety seven, we just all figured she would too. Funeral arrangements were made. My cousin asked me if I could say a few words at the service on behalf of my side of the family. Of course, I'd be honoured, I told him. Who was I kidding? I've never spoken in public in my life, I'd be terrified. But I wanted to do this for her. I loved her and yes, it would be a great honour to pay tribute to her. I had no idea how I would get through it, but I knew I had to do it.

I set about in the days before the funeral writing a eulogy for her. Never having done anything like this before, I didn't really know what I was supposed to say. So I tossed caution to the wind and decided I'd write something more light hearted than sombre.

I know that's what she would have wanted. She was one funny lady. So I composed this for her funeral:

28th June, 2007
MY AUNTY JOYCE

If I were to ask everyone here to write down one word to describe our Joyce, there would be many choices - happy, joyful, fun, loving, caring, zany, nutty.

But I'm sure an overwhelming majority would just say "funny." That is what we'll all remember most about her - her incredible sense of humour. Always laughing, always seeing the funny side of things, always making you laugh, *always* loud.

I would warn anyone meeting Joyce for the first time that they *will* go home with an aching jaw from laughing. And their ears ringing. And I was never wrong.

She's the only person I've ever known that whilst on the phone to her, you could hold it two feet away and still hear with complete clarity. In fact, you needed to hold it two feet away to protect your eardrums.

So full of joy and laughter.

While reflecting about how best to describe this amazing lady, I realized that she is a woman of contradictions - a bit like the "box of chocolates, you were never sure what you were going to get";

She could be predictable and yet spontaneous - anyone who's ever had her drag them up to dance will know what I mean; She could express her opinion and yet be non committal; Highly intelligent but incredibly.... Ditzy; Sensible or nutty as a fruitcake; Calming at times and completely anxious at others; Broad-minded yet a complete prude.

I have fond memories of her being a great cook, and an appalling one - sometimes on the same occasion. She could laugh till she cried and cry till she laughed. She could make me laugh till I cried and cry till I laughed

But to my sisters, my girls and myself she was *always:* A wonderful, devoted, caring aunt throughout our lives. . Welcoming and entertaining to everyone. There for us at all times.

God knows we've had our own challenges recently, and Joyce was there every step of the way, offering love and support on a daily basis.

She truly was the "matriarch" of our family.

Even to this end, she's caused a contradiction: For although we all feel intense sadness and sorrow at her sudden passing, we also feel an incredible joy and gratitude that we all have shared her in our lives.

Today, let's not grieve for her death, but enjoy a celebration of her life.

That's what she would have wanted.

Oh, and Joyce - Max sends his love.

****

I flew down to Sydney with one sister and one daughter - Joy was still too weak for this ordeal, and Michelle had just started a new job that week so couldn't risk asking for time off. We met my cousin at the Watson's Bay Hotel where we were to stay. He was a mess. Always so strong and in command, this had totally knocked the wind out of him. Uncle Brian was worse, he just cried and cried. Sixty years they had been married, I really feared what would happen to him now.

I was a nervous wreck. My emotions were uncontrollable. Thankfully I had asked Angie if she had anything for nerves - she'd done a lot of public speaking in her life. I knew I would need something, I was just too teary to get through this without some help. She gave me two beta-blocker tablets. I took one the morning of and another an hour before the funeral began.

We greeted people we hadn't seen for years - the usual story - you only see people at funerals. The service began. It was deeply religious. My cousin and uncle held themselves together as best they could, another cousin came forward to speak about Joyce - describing her as the 'bubbles in the champagne' at a party. It was my turn to speak. The minister had chosen a psalm from the bible for me to read! What about my lovely speech I'd prepared, I screeched to myself! It's okay, I told myself, he'll ask at the end if anyone would like to say something. I'll read it then.

I don't know what was in those beta-blockers, but I was as calm as a lizard. I came forward and read my chosen psalm with complete calmness and clarity. I returned to my seat, or the edge of my seat. I was ready to shove my hand up at the slightest hint of another chance to speak. I could have done a stand up comedy routine, I felt so relaxed. My chance never came. The minister concluded the ceremony, played some awful hymns and that was that. No music of choice. My cousin had of course chosen her favourite songs to play, as you do at a funeral. 'I just called to say I love you' would have been his number one choice, I know. Joyce loved it, she'd sing it to me every time we spoke on the phone.

I was really disappointed with the service, as I'm sure my cousin and uncle were. We are not a religious family, and this was certainly not the kind of service Joyce would have wanted. But it was done.

My perfect opportunity came at the reception afterwards. Held at the Watson's Bay hotel where Joyce and Brian were very well known, it was a lovely turn out. Old friends and friends we didn't know all mingled together. My estranged twin brother showed up as well, a brave thing for him to do I thought. The Qantas steward, we hadn't seen him for years. My niece who's always got a sharp eye for men, came up to me and asked "who is that gorgeous man over there in that Armani suit?"

"Ahhh - that's your uncle." I think she was a trifle disappointed at that knowledge. I think she fancied making a play for him.

My brother had been chatting to my ex husband for some time. I wandered over when they had a break and said "you do know that Nick and I are no longer married, don't you?" He didn't. How sad is that? Why do families do this? Estrange themselves. Such a waste.

One of my cousins bought everyone to attention and made a small toast to Joyce. He then handed over to me, explaining that I was meant to have read this at the service, but wasn't given the chance. I took the floor, unrolled my eulogy and read it with courage and conviction. And calmness, still. They all laughed at the funny bits, cried at the sad bits and congratulated me with a round of applause at the end. I was so proud of myself. It was so the right thing to do for Joyce. And everyone loved it. I rolled it up in a ribbon and presented it to Brian. It was very emotional for him.

A cousin's wife approached me afterwards and said "You were amazing. Whatever you're on, I'll have some! I know you're always a mess like me, so what was your secret?" I laughed and told her. I'll keep a sheet of those tablets handy forever.

When we flew home I emailed George with an update. "You would have been so proud of me", I told him. " I was so calm and relaxed, it was unbelievable". I copied the eulogy at the end of the email for him. "Just so you get an idea of what she was like, and what she meant to me" I explained. "And why I'm so sad at her loss".

A few hours later I received a text message from him - the first in months. "Just read your email and I've got tears rolling down my face. That was beautiful, you are incredible. I love you" it said.

The following day, the most beautiful bunch of purple and white flowers arrived for me. From George. The card read simply "love + miss you forever xxx"

Chapter 11

"Kiss and Make Up" Trip

Emails continued. I appreciated them. It showed he had at least a bit of empathy in that character of his. He knew Joyce's death had really affected me. The emails were all kept fairly light hearted, as were my replies. Until this:

"forgot to mention if you still fancy the idea of living in the med I would love it. All this travelling is very well but I miss you and never have anyone to talk to or confide in. let alone some decent lovemaking so think about it and I'll seriously make some plans love yuoooooooo gorgeous"

I sat and stared at the words for a while.

"George Harry Wilkinson! You wear me out! You are a complex man aren't you? I'm gobsmacked. You know my answer, but only if you're serious this time".

The roller coaster had started up again. Hold on, I thought to myself, it could be a rocky ride.

Before I knew it, we were talking of another holiday together. Eventually we settled on September, two months away. The last one he called the 'sex of a lifetime trip', I named this the 'kiss and make up' one. Where would I like to go? He would pay for my flight.

"Bangkok, Maldives, Barbados, or Jamaica - we could visit Hedonism, look it up on the web if you don't know what it is. I would love to go there with you. The world's your oyster. Or we could go to Spain and have a good look around. Think on it and we'll talk about it" he emailed.

What was this Hedonism he was talking about? Even the name sounded intriguing. I checked it out on the net.

I sent him a text "Please please please - can we go to Hedonism? It looks amazing! I'd only ever want to go there with you."

Oh my gosh! I didn't know places like this existed. Adults only. Open minded. Free to do whatever you please. A resort where you can let go of your inhibitions. Was I up for this kind of thing? Absolutely! Why not! As long as you don't cross any boundaries with each other.

Within four days he'd booked it. A week in Jamaica at Hedonism resort. All inclusive. He forwarded me the email confirming the booking. "Thank you, thank you, thank you. I love you so much" I emailed back to him.

More plans were made around this week. Never one to pass an opportunity, I thought why can't we do more than just that? Why not go to Spain to look around as well?

I certainly wasn't going to fly all the way over there for just a week. The Jamaica holiday flew out from London. I was thrilled - I'd never been to England before. All those trips to Europe in the last six years, and I'd never ventured to the UK. And who better to show me London than an Englishman?

My flight was booked. Four days in London before flying out to Jamaica, then back for a couple of weeks in Spain, then we take it from there. I was back on cloud nine again. Well I did say this was a roller coaster ride with him didn't I?

Collecting my mail one day in the village, I ran into my friend Damien who always had time to hear about my love life with my Yorkshire man. He'd known about the last heartbreak. He'd been hearing about George for the last two years. Had met him at my office cocktail party. "Darling, if you want to keep this man, you're going to have to just pick up sticks and move over there. Land on his doorstep. Then you'll find out if he really means what he says. Sounds like he can't really live without you. And how could he? Look at you, how could he resist you? Love you, gotta go."

Darling Damien. Always said it like it was. Why couldn't I have a man like him? Then I remembered why. "You've got one of those yucky vagina things, darling" he'd once replied when I asked that question to him. Shame.

He was right. I need to just do it. Pack up and stay over there. That would really force his hand. I was making it too easy for him living a million miles away.

Chapter 12

Underpants and Carving Knives

While my mind was processing this new decision, I took a weekend off and flew down to Sydney to visit my uncle. Angie came with me, she had a new man in her life from Lancashire who was arriving in a week. She was scouting to find some interesting sights to show him and wasn't all that familiar with Sydney. I'd been anxious to see how Brian was coping in the house alone.

Hiring a car at the airport, I set the sat nav for Watson's Bay. Normally I would have known my way out there, but there were new motorways from the airport that I wasn't familiar with. Not a great lover of these devices, I had no choice but to trust it on this occasion. Take a tip from me - they don't work in tunnels. I found myself heading onto the six lanes across the Harbour Bridge not once, but three times before I lost it and pulled the damn thing out of it's socket. Every time I went under the same tunnel, it lost its bearings and directed me onto a one way street that took me over the bridge. Three lots of tolls it cost me! Not familiar with North Sydney at all, I then had to work out a way to get back onto the bridge to cross back to the city side. In the end I just followed my nose and found my own way there. With no help from Angie I might add.

I'd booked to stay at the Watson's Bay Hotel again. This hotel is the best kept secret in Sydney according to my cousin. I have to agree. Very reasonably priced, with harbour views across to the city, and a stroll down to the jetty for a ferry into town. Oh, and a world famous Doyle's restaurant on its doorstep as well.

A visit to Brian was first on the agenda. I picked up some nibbles and wine on the way and headed on over. I was eager to show Angie the house, it perched on a rock ledge (even had aboriginal paintings in a cave underneath) with the most incredible views from Bondi Beach right across to the Harbour Bridge and the Opera House. The first ever advertisement for a Hills Hoist was filmed from their backyard showing the panorama. Tour coaches used to pull up outside to show passengers the views from their position. Joyce often suggested serving tea and scones on her front lawn. During the bi-centennial celebrations in 1988, our entire family spent the day in their house. To our amazement, people started arriving and spreading blankets on the front lawn in readiness for the fireworks. She could have made a killing with tea and scones. If only she knew how to cook them! That day was amazing for us, we couldn't see a glimpse of water on the harbour for the boats that had crammed together on it.

Brian appeared to be coping fairly well, I was pleased to see. He had a wonderful circle of friends who were constantly calling on him, but he looked haggard. A heavy wine drinker, I suspected his intake had increased since Joyce's passing. The house had deteriorated since I'd last seen it a few years earlier. His son was right, he couldn't stay there on his own. He wasn't capable of taking care of it anymore. It was to be sold and Brian move to Melbourne near his son. I had to agree this would be the best solution. So this was to be my last visit ever to a house that held wonderful memories for me. Brian would be very comfortable from the sale of this home. I expected it would sell in excess of three million dollars, probably to a developer.

Angie and I left the house late afternoon, Brian looked tired. I took her on a nostalgia drive through Vaucluse where I spent my childhood. My nana's house was still there - more wonderful memories - her road led down to cliffs that remain unfenced to this day. I showed Angie the gully that Brian and my father used to climb down to go fishing off the rocks - until my father fell down the gully and broke nearly every bone in his body. He had to be rescued, of course they didn't use helicopters back then. Then Vaucluse House and Parsley Bay - a tiny little beach on the harbour that Joyce used to take me to when I was little. It was quite a sentimental journey for me, and a little sad. No, a lot.

Dinner at the famous Doyle's restaurant. A tad expensive, but I couldn't bring Angie to Watson's Bay and not dine there. Doyle's *is* Watson's Bay.

A day in the city was planned for the Sunday. We caught the ferry across to Circular Quay and wandered around. The Museum of Contemporary

Art at the Quay had a Latin American exhibition on - a banner of Che Guevara hung out front. This could be intriguing, we thought. An understatement.

As we exited the lift to the first floor, we were faced with our first exhibition - a pair of men's underpants (white, full brief) with gold embroidered emblems down the front and crotch areas; there was a series of photos - one was a needle and thread with the caption "my mother told me not to sew in the dark or I'd go blind"; a room full of kitchen carving knives hanging from the ceiling (this area was roped off, in case someone decided on the touch and feel approach); but the piece de resistance was a full length evening gown made of a fabric that resembled human skin with anuses all over it! (Yes, as in arseholes). Of course it was accessorised with matching shoes and handbag. And not to forget the man who has everything, there was also a soccer ball covered in the same fabric. Gives a whole new meaning to the phrase 'kicked in the arse', doesn't it? I have to tell you, we needed a drink after that little visit. Then on to a puppet maker shop in the underground caverns of the Rocks, hundreds and hundreds of the weirdest puppets and marionettes you've ever seen. And a charming French man who offered to take us on a guided tour of the Rocks, if only someone could mind his shop for him.

We wandered over to the Opera House for a few photo opportunities before heading back on the ferry. Our time was up and we headed back to the airport - no sat nav this time.

I had roughly eight weeks till the 'kiss and make up' trip. My townhouse went back on the market and sold for asking price to the first couple that viewed it. A record price for the complex, I was pretty chuffed. This time, it must have been meant to be. I extended settlement day to coincide with my departure date, leaving myself a few days to get my furniture into storage and tie up loose ends.

I didn't know how long I would be away for. I'd booked a return ticket with a date that could be changed. Hopefully, I wasn't going to need it, I secretly admitted to myself. Nicole could take over the business if I decided to stay - she was welcome to it. It was becoming so stressful, never knowing when your next sale would happen.

Catch ups with friends took up a lot of my time. They all knew that I wouldn't be back for some time if things worked out with George this time. They were cautiously optimistic for me. Actually, if I really admit it to myself, they probably thought I was a fool giving him another chance. I would probably have thought the same of one of them. But I truly loved this man. He was under my skin. I had to give him another go.

Chapter 13

Archangels

Departure day had arrived. I was so excited. A fair amount of trepidation too about what I was about to embark on. Five weeks I'd be gone, maybe longer if things work out, I told my daughters. They were happy for me in an odd sort of way, even though I knew secretly they disapproved of me seeing George again. But they didn't let it show.

I looked great. Regular workouts at the gym plus my yoga and swimming had trimmed and toned me. Nicole had become my personal trainer. She pushed me beyond my limits, had me running up steep hills at the golf course nearby. Perhaps she was trying to kill me so I couldn't go to this man, I wondered. I was down to a weight I hadn't reached in twenty years. I was even able to buy a pair of size 10 Tommy Hilfiger jeans! Now that's an achievement!

After a non descript flight, I touched down in Heathrow Airport. First stop, the bathroom to change into something that would really show off my sexy new figure.

I planned the outfit for weeks - wanted to be casual but still turn heads - one in particular. A clingy white top, knee length light denim jeans with a turned up cuff, trendy silver belt and a pair of really cute peep toe, red and white stripe high heels and matching bag. I'd made sure I'd slept on the plane for the last leg, and with a full face of make-up hurriedly applied in the ladies toilets, I joined the queue in customs.

What a queue! I never imagined how busy this airport would be. I messaged George to let him know I could be half an hour at least. "You won't miss me - I'm the only blonde in a sea of black hair and turbans", I advised him. Almost every person in the 'non EU passenger' line was Indian or Pakistani. Mass migration. Was it always like this? I began to wish I'd left the shoe changing till after I passed through customs. These little red and white numbers weren't built for comfort. I shifted continuously, they were killing me. Finally my turn. After the usual interrogation from the customs officer, my passport was stamped and I was through! My heart was racing, those butterflies were back again. One last touch up of the hair and a bra adjustment and I passed through the doors.

There he was! He'd seen me in the mirrors before I came through the door, so had broken through the barrier and greeted me in the centre of the walkway. It was wonderful, back in each other's arms again. He kissed all my lipstick off, much to his amusement. It was probably smeared all over my face by now. I didn't care. I was so happy to see him. He stood back and looked at me. "Wow!! You look gorgeous!"

My hard work had paid off. That was all I needed to hear.

We made our way outside. He'd organised for his mate to pick us up he said, and take us into London to our hotel. We spent the next half hour looking for a white car, he was late.

"Is that him?" I pointed to a little white hatch back across the road.

"No, it's a bit bigger than that". So I repeated this questioning every time I noticed a white car. He made a couple of calls. Finally, he spotted his lift.

He'd ordered a stretch limousine to pick me up! How romantic! Champagne, chocolates, the works. I loved him for that. He pointed out some famous landmarks along the way. We snogged for most of the journey. He'd booked us into the Strand Palace Hotel. It was perfect. Another bottle of champagne on ice in our room. Gosh, much more of this and I'd be out like a light. I'd just spent the last 24 hours flying.

First things first though. The lovemaking. It was wonderful, as always. He then let me have a bit of a sleep before we ventured out to dinner. And my first taste of England.

London was fantastic! I loved everything about it. Why had I taken so long to discover it, I thought to myself? Although, being there with a man I loved who knew all the best places to show me made it more amazing than if I'd been there on my own, I realized.

George was a brilliant tour guide. We caught black cabs, red buses and trains on the tube everywhere. He planned an itinerary with meticulous detail for me. I was impressed. My only stipulation

I'd made was for him to take me to see Phantom of the Opera. I'd never seen the stage production, just the movie so it was to hold a special place in me to see it with him, in London. He was into the theatre, I knew this. He'd acted in plays himself. So I knew it wouldn't be agony for him to sit through a musical. I'll give him his due though - he had seen it before and had fallen asleep half way through (after an afternoon of drinking with his mates), so he didn't particularly like it, so he thought. This time 'round he loved it, and was glad I'd requested it. We had a lovely night, all dressed up - he in a suit and me in a little black dress and red overcoat- like proper theatre goers should dress.

Arriving back at the hotel, we enjoyed a Bailey's before making our way to our room. I'd been waiting for the right moment to give George my gift. That moment was now, after such a special night. I presented him with a ring. Silver and titanium, it was beautiful. (I think I'd secretly been hoping he'd give me a gift first and didn't want to rain on his parade - at this stage I'd already spoilt one surprise.)

He was speechless. This was a first for him!

"This is the loveliest thing anyone's ever given me" was all he could manage to say.

He loved it, genuinely loved it. It was a really classy ring. Sadly, it was about five sizes too small for him.

I didn't realize how big his hands were. I should have - you know what they say about big hands….

"It won't be a problem gorgeous" I explained.

"The jeweller did say he could make another one if we needed, so don't worry. I'll email him."

We were disappointed. He wanted to wear it straight away. He placed it back in it's velvet pouch and packed it into a zippered section inside his suitcase.

We thought no more about it.

Our four days were really full - he'd thought of everything. A ride on the London Eye followed by a cruise on the Thames, a day in the Tower of London. He showed me the Houses of Parliament and Westminster Abbey. I was admiring the carvings and masonry on the arches of the Abbey.

"Look," I pointed out to him " those adorable little angels there - *Arch*angels!" I exclaimed smugly.

"Easy tiger. I'll do the jokes here" he replied laughing.

He'd planned a couple of surprises too, he'd told me. (One being the limo on arrival.) But on we went - Covent Garden, Portobello Road markets and Notting Hill, Hyde Park and Kensington Palace, afternoon tea in Harrods, Fortnum and Masons, Hamley's Toy Store. Just as well I was fit, I'd never have kept up with him otherwise.

And a champagne in the Savoy Hotel - fifteen pounds a glass!

We sat in a café for a coffee break one morning. A red double decker bus had stopped outside.

"Look, that poster on the bus says Buckingham Palace is open till the 29th! I thought you told me it closed earlier this month. We *haven't* missed it!" I exclaimed.

He looked at me in disbelief. Then hung his head and shook it from side to side in utter disappointment.

"I know, I've got tickets for us" he said dejectedly.

"That was the surprise I had for you" he continued.

Oh no! I'd spoilt his surprise! I felt terrible. I could see how disappointed he was.

"What were the chances of that bus pulling up there, and you even noticing the poster?" he groaned. I felt really bad.

He got over it though when he saw my excitement and delight when we did go into the Palace the next day. I was like a little girl in a doll's shop. It was wonderful. The Palace was wonderful. I was so grateful he'd taken me. I was absolutely overwhelmed by everything about London, wide eyed like a child. George loved this aspect about me - he enjoyed seeing me enjoying myself.

We explored Leicester Square at night, and of course visited a few comedy clubs. One of the comedian's was doing a very clever skit about the dangers of predictive text on mobile phones. Everyone was in stitches as he relayed some of the funnier messages that had gone wrong with predictive text. He questioned if anyone else had the same experiences - things like "I can't wait to _kick_ your _puppy_" to your girlfriend - the two of us were laughing and nodding to him, embarrassingly admitting that yes, George had sent me that message once. I'll leave you to work that one out.

My first taste of London had been a huge success. What a fantastic city. I loved the cabbies, they were so friendly and funny. Everyone was friendly actually. And so polite. It was a lovely change from some of the countries I'd visited.

Our time was up and we were off on the next part of our adventure - Jamaica!

Chapter 14

Jamaica Mon

Packing up for our journey to Jamaica, the zipper on George's bag packed it in. We bought some duct-tape and strapped it tightly closed. What a useful invention - I don't know how the world would get by without duct-tape. My ex-husband once held one of his car's together with the stuff. He'd duct-tape anything.

When we arrived at Montego Bay airport (by the way, don't ever make Miami your choice as a transfer airport . It was horrendous), we had to make a dash for it across the tarmac. They were in the middle of a tropical storm. The baggage handlers wouldn't unload the luggage till the rain stopped. We all had to wait around, curiously watching the terminal around the baggage carousel filling with water. By the time the carousel finally cranked into action an hour later, we were wading through two inches of water.

My suitcase arrived. Every other passenger's suitcase arrived. George's didn't. The carousel ground to a halt. The terminal emptied - of people, not water. George was not a happy chappy. Lots of paperwork followed. Our resort address was noted. They would deliver his case when they located it. "When might that be?" we enquired.

Could take a few days, they told us. We caught our transfer coach to our resort.

We were starving. We hadn't eaten since lunchtime on the flight. It was now around ten at night. Luckily we were able to grab a meal just as the resort's buffet restaurant was closing, they were very obliging. From what we could see so far, this was a lovely resort with a lively atmosphere. We were in for a fun week, we could tell already. Apart from George's missing luggage, that is. Unpacking didn't take long…..

Our room was fabulous. George had chosen well. It was on the first floor overlooking one of the pools below. I liked that it was not on the ground floor, safer from a security point of view. The shower over the spa bath was beside a louvred window, so you could watch the activities in the pool while you showered, or they could watch the activities in the shower if you chose. The bedroom was colourful as is Jamaica. Tropical prints on all the soft furnishings. And a huge mirror on the ceiling above the bed. "Well, *that's* nice" we both thought. We flopped into bed, it had been a long day.

Unbeknownst to me, George had been up a few times during the night with diarrhoea. How sweet that he hadn't disturbed me with his ills, I thought. Very unman-like, most men have a need to let the world know when they're feeling a little off colour. I woke in the morning to the sound of him throwing his heart up in the bathroom. As he snuggled back into bed beside me, I had to make a dash for the bathroom. It was my turn. One toilet, two cases of diarrhea and vomiting. We got to know each other intimately over the next four days, I have to say. There was nothing we didn't know or hadn't seen about each other by the end of this ordeal! It was awful, we were both so ill, and became so weak.

We thought back. On the flight from Miami, I had commented on the ham sandwiches we had been served. On opening the sandwich, I noticed that half of the meat had turned that odd brownish colour that indicates it shouldn't be eaten. George smelled it, it had no smell. "No, it's fine" he said. No, it wasn't, we now realised.

In the initial stages, I faired slightly better than George. We had managed to drag ourselves down to breakfast that first morning, but all we fancied was some orange juice. Which didn't stay down. I left George sleeping while I wandered over to the on-site store for some essentials for him. He had no clothes, no toiletries, nothing. They were somewhere en route between Miami and Jamaica. It was so easy buying these essentials for a man - a shaver and a toothbrush was all he needed. No make-up, skin care, hair products that we women couldn't live without for more than half a day. I chose a nice pair of shorts and the 'most tasteful' resort t-shirt I could find. Didn't bother with underpants, he liked going commando style.

The next two days followed the same pattern - venture down to the restaurant, grab a plate and fill it with a lettuce leaf, some cucumber and tomato that then didn't get eaten. Lemonade was all we dared to drink, even that had trouble staying down. Then back to our room for a sleep to recover from the exertion. An occasional venture out to check out the resort, a quick game of table tennis or pool and back to bed again. And of course the races to the toilet, sometimes needing to use it at the same time. We had to request more toilet paper. By our third morning, we decided we probably should go see the resort nurse. Quite an elderly Jamaican lady, she was kind and caring. She only had to look at us to see we were both really ill. She immediately called for a doctor and took stool samples. The results would take three weeks. Three weeks! We could be dead by then!

She correctly diagnosed gastroenteritis, caused from food poisoning. The doctor confirmed this when he arrived. At two hundred and forty American dollars each for his call out visit, we stopped short of letting him look at both of us. We both had the same symptoms, so George made him check me out and prescribe something that we could both take. We were both given strict instructions that if we hadn't improved by nightfall, we were to go to hospital immediately. This was serious. The tablets worked almost straight away. By dinner time, we had recovered well enough to have our first real food since that first night. Our nurse was lovely, she checked on us every day and monitored our improvement.

Finally we were able to start having fun. George's suitcase eventually arrived on this day as well. Well, a semblance of it anyway. It looked sad, like a derelict living on the streets. It was battered and dirty, most of the duct-tape had disappeared, replaced with packing tape and all held together with a luggage strap of sorts. Our hearts jumped out of our mouths. What was missing we wondered? He quickly pulled everything apart. All his clothes were still there, his toiletries and some fairly valuable autographs that he had hidden in a book were all there. Who brings valuable autographs away on a holiday I wondered? Why? But this was George, it bore no explanation.

The only items missing were his beloved Jo Malone aftershave, and the ring. He was devastated and so was I. About the ring, not the aftershave. And we were annoyed with ourselves, not each other. Why hadn't he just given it straight back to me for safe keeping in my handbag? It had to be sent back to Australia to be replaced, so yes he should have just given it back to me. No use beating ourselves up about it now. It was done. And it was gone. It had cost me a bloody fortune too, he coaxed out of me what I had paid for it. He felt even worse. Never mind, let's not let it spoil our holiday, I told him. Not a good sign, I thought to myself.

Hedonism was everything it professed to be. It was the most exhilarating, liberating and fun place I'd ever been to. The staff were incredible and all gorgeous. Jamaicans are hot, with the most amazing bums, we discovered. They all went by assumed names like 'Storm', 'Prince', 'Sapphire' etc. Activities organisers, waiters, cleaners by day and entertainers at night. The evening entertainment was fantastic. Something different every night, headed up by an extremely camp 'lady boy' who was much more comfortable in a figure hugging mini dress doing Cher impersonations than his daytime uniform of shorts and resort shirt. Known as 'Cruise', his personality was intoxicating - he really knew how to entertain his guests.

We laid down some ground rules before we got into enjoying ourselves. If either of us fancied some 'swinging' we had to consider what the other one was getting as their end of the bargain. Not many of the couples here were 'evenly' matched, we noticed. In other words, if one was good looking, there partner was butt ugly. We hadn't openly discussed the possibility of swinging, but we both knew what this resort was about. We were both adventurous, we knew that much about each other.

As it turned out, nothing like that happened. We were both too into each other again to want to venture down that path.

There were games and competitions of every kind, all leaning toward the risqué side of course. This was Hedonism after all. I found myself on stage participating in these games on more occasions than I care to remember. I'd left my inhibitions behind in Australia. George had that effect on me. Ever the comedian, he never had a problem with making a fool of himself. It was rubbing off. My friends and colleagues wouldn't have recognised me - they only ever saw a self controlled, sober, slightly posh and snobby woman who always kept her behaviour in check because of her profession.

Even I didn't recognise myself. I found myself up on stage with George and five other couples, embarking in a competition of who could come up with the most number of sexual positions on a mattress on the stage in sixty seconds. We won! We were the oldest couple in the competition. Ahhh, the benefits of age and experience!

Most nights after the entertainment, we would end up in the piano bar for karaoke. I couldn't bring myself to do it, and still can't. Something about being handed a microphone turns me to stone. Not George. Of course. This was the first time I'd seen him sing. He sang a fantastic rendition of 'Maggie May' that was to become his swan song between us. And then sang 'Love is in the Air'- made famous by an Aussie singer - to me, meaning every word of it. The audience loved it, it was very romantic.

We met Suzannah and her sister Mary, African-American ladies from Alabama. Suzannah was a repeat customer, coming here for short breaks for a 'piece of action' as she called it.

In a serious relationship back home she ex-plained, but needed more excitement in her life. My kind of woman! Her sister Mary, hadn't had sex in twenty years. I figured Suzannah was maybe thirty and her sister mid forties, pushing fifty at most. She kept referring to her son and his wife though. So I had to ask - "how old *are* you?" To our amazement, she was fifty two and Mary was seventy! She was almost my age! Oh my god. And oh my god at what she was wearing! A gold crocheted, ultra short, string dress with nothing under it. Nothing. She took to the stage - or the top of the grand piano actually - and belted out Shirley Bassey's 'Fever'. She had an incredible voice. And an incredible body. The men were transfixed, George included. Her dress kept riding up every time she swung her arms about mid chorus, exposing her bare fanny to everyone. She didn't care. No one else cared. She was amazing. She made a play for me, to my surprise. I think she would have liked a threesome with George and I. I'd never even entertained the thought of being with a woman, and wasn't about to. I was adventurous, but not that adventurous!

We became good friends with them though. Mary was hilarious, she had a strong southern drawl and was a really funny lady. Hadn't been with a man for twenty years; she was so lovely I was even prepared to lend George out to her to blow away the cobwebs, so to speak. She would have loved it. We thought about it. But didn't offer.

George really played up to her though, using his hilarious negro accent to tease her about her lack of sex. "watch you mean woman, you haven't had no black sausage all them years! Why, yor pussy must be closed shut! Cobwebs at the door. Let me get my broom out, I'll sweep em away" he joked with her. She loved it. Every time we saw them he adopted this negro 'speak' to her. Never laughed so much in her life, she told us at the end of their stay. George had made this the best holiday she'd ever had. That was nice.

One of the nights later that week was a talent show. George and Suzannah enrolled for it, naturally enough. I'd rallied round our many new found friends to make sure they didn't miss it. George and I knew that this American audience would struggle understanding his broad Yorkshire accent, so he needed as much support as he could get. Rent a crowd, kind of. We needn't have worried. His comedy routine went over a treat, they loved him. Then came Suzannah. She sang 'At Last', the famous Etta James song. She wore a stunning white and silver fringe dress. She kept her fanny covered this time. She was incredible. Brought the house down. She won.

During the week we were there, I was lucky enough to find that the resort had two contests happening. One was an all male dance competition, with heats on each night, narrowing down to a finals night. I'd already picked the winner. So had every other woman. We were smitten. 'Ricco' from Puerto Rico had the most amazing moves, sexing up to the audience. Beautiful aqua 'come to bed' eyes, he was stunningly handsome. Even the men were falling for him. Gorgeous body, gorgeous face. He was sex on legs. Even had a fantastic personality, I was lucky enough to find out. We'd chat to him each night before the show. God, I just wanted to jump him!

The second contest was 'Mr Caribbean'. Yes girls, I'd struck gold. Poor George, there were to be no such contests for the guys to enjoy. My recommendations to anyone who ever sees this contest advertised - max out your credit card and get on a plane! Twelve 'god's' strutted their stuff for four nights. It was like a beauty pageant. They sang, they danced, they melted our hearts. The women that is. Probably some men too. Really nice guys, they joined in with the activities during the day's. Two of them joined us on a glass bottomed boat, out snorkelling in the bay. Mr Jamaica had been an Olympic swimmer, Mr Barbados his mate had been a diver. One night they all wore tuxedos - mmm, yum - another night swimwear. All hail the Speedo!

Their final night was the famous 'Toga' night in the resort. Now picture this - twelve drop-dead-gorgeous black men of all shades from cappuccino to strong black, with bodies the likes of which I'd never seen before and buns of steel, all smooth and shiny and muscley. Then wrap each of them in a tiny piece of white sheeting, twisting and tie-ing it in various styles just covering their manhood, and parade them on stage to an audience of pissed, horny women who've just spent a week of unadulterated pleasure in and out of the bedroom. Got that image clearly in your mind? Then you can imagine how the night ended. Or erupted would be a more apt description. I don't remember who won. It didn't matter. That vision of my twelve disciples is etched in my mind forever. Lucky me.

After losing three days to illness, we wanted to make up for lost time. We explored every square inch of the resort. We wandered over to the 'nude' area. We'd only hung out in the 'prude' area as it was called, while we were ill. What a revelation. There was a huge pool complete with waterfall and grotto, and a swim up pool bar. Beyond this was a lovely little palm fringed beach and cove. It was beautiful.

And very well policed. Signs indicated the approach to this nude area of the resort, with warnings that photography was strictly forbidden. Security guards patrolled everywhere, even on the beach. It was quite an absurd scene, seeing fully clothed guards chatting to naked guests, and turning a blind eye to couples making love on swinging hammocks scattered throughout the grounds.

We'd found our 'Utopia'. It took no convincing for us to disrobe and dive right in. And the people who hung out there were the greatest fun. No one cared what shape you were in, they just swam up to a stool beside us at the bar and chatted away, not giving our 'bits' a second glance. It was exhilarating. We had a ball. We made some really great friends. The staff entertained us each afternoon. There were best bum and wet t-shirt competitions. This was hilarious - naked women donning t-shirts with their bums and fannies exposed - to be judged on the best look in a wet t-shirt! Cocktail mixing competitions - we each added an ingredient to a cocktail in the pool bar, and the barman then poured it into our throats and down our naked bodies until we declared a favourite. It then became the cocktail of the day.

Every night we ended up with bottles of Jamaica Rum that we'd won for various competitions we'd entered around the resort. We had won so many bottles of this white rum that we gave Mary half a dozen bottles to take home. She was delighted, she was a really poor woman from the South. We were really happy to have met her and her sister. Never did find out if Mary got her cobwebs blown away.

Not wanting to disturb a couple we spotted having sex on the beach, we waited till they'd finished before plunging into the cove for a swim. Gosh, it was so invigorating swimming naked in the sea. A Jamaican man sitting on the rocks was trying to sell us some pot as we fondled each other in the water. A guard soon rid us of our intruder. Then it was our turn to make love on a sun-bed on the beach.

We sunbathed by the pool, making new friends every day. I'd never seen so many tits and cocks in one place. I felt pretty good about my own body after seeing some of the shapes here. But they didn't care, that was the lovely part of it. A Swedish man wore a gold cock ring with a chain attached to his balls - I'd never seen this sort of jewellery before. Perhaps George might like that as a replacement for the lost ring? I wondered. Every time I glanced over, his wife was playing with him. This kind of fondling was openly accepted. Not full on sex however. Not around the pool. The beach and the hammocks were fine though.

They were such a great crowd. We fitted in really well. George entertained them constantly with his repertoire of jokes. On the day that the male dancers were leaving in their coach, our 'group' planned a send off at the front of the resort. We all lined up around the fountain in the roundabout, and dropped our towels as the coach circled us, wagging our bare bums at these gorgeous guys. And Ricco. What a hoot! Was this the same demure Judi from Australia? The one with the posh job and the posh car who lived in the posh suburb as George always said? I couldn't believe I'd just done that! But I loved it!

On one of our days in the nude pool, a black American couple came along. They were very good looking. When they hopped into the pool, everyone's jaw dropped. He had the biggest cock any of us had ever seen. It wasn't even erect. The men automatically reached down to cover up their own packages, and the women gulped. It made your eyes water. Turned out they were getting married in the resort the following day. They were lovely. And they had abstained from sex while they'd been here, to make it right for their wedding. He must have been ready to burst. All us women had the same thought - pick me, pick me!

The next day we all gathered round - clothed - to watch the ceremony. She looked beautiful in a simple white dress, he in white slacks and shirt. The marriage was taking place in a little gazebo adorned with flowers that jutted out over the water. It was an idyllic setting. They had no friends or family with them, which we thought was sad. The celebrant came over and asked George and me if we'd like to be witnesses to their marriage. We were honoured. And amused. We didn't know them from Noah, would probably never hear from them again and we were about to sign our names on the marriage certificate! This posed a bit of a dilemma - do I sign my own surname or George's? Everyone thought we were married, George always introduced me as his wife. "You decide" he said simply. I signed - Judi Wilkinson.

I think we were chosen as we were the only half decently dressed couple in attendance. George wore his white Hedonism t-shirt (I think this was a deciding factor) but I only had my bikini on with a see-through sarong slung around my bottom. So we now appeared in some strangers' wedding photo's as their witnesses, decidedly underdressed for such an occasion. George snogged the bride. I kissed the groom. Lucky girl, all us women thought. Wish we could be in your shoes tonight. Or bed.

We would meet up with some of our 'nude' friends for drinks after dinner. The usual 'I didn't recognise you with your clothes on' jokes followed. One of the nights was a pyjama party up in the disco. I'd prepared for this before I came away, and had selected a cute black and white polka dot nightie and knickers set that was quite sexy. Not sexy enough. I felt overdressed to say the least. There were corsets and suspenders, fishnet stockings, g-strings galore, crutchless knickers, you name it - it was there. Even the men wore a variety of g-strings and cock covers. We felt quite 'prude' in comparison. We danced the night away. Sometime during the course of the evening I lost my knickers, George had removed them to wear on his head and they were never seen again.

There was a fabulous water slide in the resort. Part of it was see-through, lit with coloured lights and passed through the disco. We had seen bodies flying past us all night. It didn't open till midnight. By two in the morning and plied with alcohol, we decided it would be fun for us. Leaving our clothes at the bottom, we climbed the stairs with the others, all naked. Gosh, this place was such fun. Disneyland for adults. We came down the slide half a dozen times and kept going back for more. The guard who had been policing it and spacing us between slides took a break. "Lets go down together", I coaxed George. "The guard won't know."

We went back for another turn. Again, we slid down together. Me in front, George sitting at back of me. We built up quite a speed, being thrown up high on one side of the slide and then the other. We were having a great time. Until - bang! - my head hit the wall just before the end. George saw it - and heard it. He reached into the water as soon as we hit it and reefed me out and onto the side of the pool. Grabbed our clothes and a towel each and took me immediately back to our room. When we got there, I had an enormous egg on the side of my forehead.

I was okay, I assured him. We were both pretty drunk, so it numbed any pain I might have been feeling. I slept through the night fine. The next morning George was back in the bathroom. We still hadn't fully recovered from our illness. As I laid in bed, the room started spinning. Not the slow spinning you experience when you're drunk, I'd sobered up well and truly by now. This was speed spinning, and everything that was in the room behind me - a mirror and shelf behind the bed with flowers, a radio and other knick-knacks on it plus the wardrobe doors, appeared in front of me. And spun and spun around me at high speed. I freaked out. I screamed out to George.

He didn't hear me. Something told me to sit up. The spinning stopped. Every time I went to put my head back on the pillow it started again. George finally came out of the bathroom. I was crying, it really scared me. I had concussion. I knew it, George knew it. But we couldn't let the nurse know it. She would have definitely sent me off to hospital this time. I didn't want that. We'd already lost enough time here being sick. So I slept sitting up with pillows propped around me, with George keeping a close eye on me all day.

I was fine by the end of the day, our friends a little concerned though. I got the usual lectures. Yes, when we got back to London I'd see a doctor. Blimey, at the prices they charge here, it would have used up all our holiday money I told them. Poor George. He was totally freaking out about how he would explain it to my daughters if anything came of this.

"Well it's like this girls. Your mother and I were sliding naked down a slide......" Oh dear, it wouldn't look good.

Sadly, our week drew to a close. We'd made many friends, exchanged email addresses, promised to stay in touch. You know, the usual things you do on holiday.

With George's homeless bag taped back together again, we headed back to London.

No naked send off for us though - we were a tad disappointed.

We sang Bob Marley songs all the way to the airport. Goodbye Jamaica! "Thank you for a holiday of a lifetime" we chorused.

Chapter 15

Baileys and Bruises

Our arrival back in London went a lot smoother than the previous one in Jamaica. No lost luggage, no flooding terminals, no food poisoning - so far. We had organised to fly straight to Spain the same day. We caught the transfer coach from Heathrow to Gatwick Airport and linked up with our flight to Alicante. Amazingly, George's bag had held together which was just as well because we didn't have time to buy another one. We'd take care of that in Calpe.

My friend Angie had kindly let us have her flat for as long as we needed it, she wasn't planning any trips over there for a while. We agreed on a nominal price that would cover expenses for her. We weren't sure what our plans were yet. George knew my townhouse had been sold and my belongings were in storage. It was his call.

We arrived in Alicante and picked up a hire car. Settled into the flat in Calpe and went out for dinner. We'd been flying all day so we were pretty tired. The following day we went grocery shopping together. George took a photo of me pulling the cute little shopping basket on wheels. We both were very relaxed doing the shopping and found that we shared the same taste in foods and grocery items. We were very compatible in all forms of domesticity we discovered, and both neat freaks. We soon settled into some semblance of a daily routine while we made plans.

Was I prepared to stay over here with him? He asked me. "You've got me as long as you want" I replied. We were so much in love again. And incredibly comfortable with each other. Well, after a bout of gastroenteritis together, you would be wouldn't you?

It was during this time in Calpe that George confessed to me the real reason he had left Australia. He had overstayed his visa and they had caught up with him. He had to leave. It had devastated him, he truly loved it there. I was shocked, but I did understand why he hadn't told me before. It was embarrassing to admit it. He had been given a three year ban before they would consider letting him return.

George had been to Cyprus earlier that year and had loved it. He had thrown in his job with the exhibition company just prior to me arriving in London. He was tired of the travelling. Would I like to check out Cyprus before we decide on a place to settle? Of course I would. "I don't mind where I live as long as I'm with you" I replied like a love struck teenager. As long as it's got plenty to do, good beaches and some job prospects as well, I thought to myself.

So the plan was we would stay in Calpe for three weeks, catch up with my friends Lauren and Kim who I had arranged to meet, then fly to Cyprus. Lauren was spending her birthday at her sister's in Torrevieja, south of Alicante and had organised a party for us all to attend. How lovely it is to meet up with friends from home half way across the world.

So our days turned into weeks. It was an odd situation to be in - we weren't really on holiday any more but neither of us had a job either, so it was getting a bit tedious. We filled in our days reading the papers, going for walks and making love in the afternoons. Gary from Sinatra's welcomed us back, we found a few quiz nights that we became regulars at. The restaurant we'd had the funny night in had closed down. We visited Benidorm again. Another hilarious night. A couple of the comedians remembered us from last time. We were a memorable couple -George the heckler with the Australian wife - weren't too many of them around.

About a week into our Calpe stay, I was putting on make-up and noticed a dark mark on my eyelid. I went out to George to show him.

"What do you think this is?" I asked. As he looked carefully at it, he started laughing. In the natural light, he could see that it was part of a bruise that went from above my eyebrow down to my cheekbone and right across to my temple. A result of the bang to my head! Then he stopped laughing when he realized what it would look like to everyone. I had a black eye! How was he going to explain this away? Especially to my girls. Now I was the one laughing.

On my way to the beauty salon one day while George caught up on some much needed sleep, a woman came running up behind me. "Senora, senora!" she was calling to me. She grabbed me on the arm. "That man is trying to catch your attention" she explained. "Where?" I looked around. It was Elias, my Spanish toy boy from my first time in Calpe, eighteen months ago. I waved to him but he was driving. Thank goodness, I thought. Before I knew it, he was running up behind me. How happy he was to see me. How glad I was that I was alone. Awkward moment, that could have been. His English hadn't improved much, but he made it clear he wanted to pick up our little fling again. "You like sexa again with me, si?" he asked. "No, afraid not" I exclaimed. I explained to him that I was here with my future husband so no, I would not be picking up where we left off. "That little old bald man I saw you with the other day?" he asked in his broken English. How flattering for me! "Why are you with him?" he asked. "You could have someone young like me" he went on. "That's very sweet Elias, but I am in love with this man and we are together now. Please don't try and see me again" I finished. I prayed I wouldn't run into him again, especially with George. I never did luckily.

Lauren's birthday party night arrived. We picked Kim up from her beachfront hotel in Torrevieja and wound our way through a maze of rabbit warrens to the house for pre dinner drinks. Lauren's sister lived in an 'urbanization', which had appealed to me as a place to live with George. Until we got to this one. There were hundreds of little town houses and villa's all crammed in together with nothing to do but become nosey neighbours I suspected. Not my cup of tea, and George knew it.

What a great night though. Lauren met George for the first time. He was on his best behaviour while we enjoyed champagne for an hour or so before heading into town for dinner. Lulled me into a false sense of security with his polite demeanour. They wanted to know all about our holiday in Jamaica. We gave them a brief rundown, leaving out the parts we thought would shock them. The nude pool, the 'sex positions' competition, the naked water slide etc. Cleaned the story up a bit. It still made an entertaining tale with our illness and the bang to my head.

Dinner was in a lovely Italian restaurant in town. There were about fourteen of us spread over two tables. George must have told every joke he knew, they just rolled off his tongue. When he get's going he can't stop. I never understood how he could remember them all, I would try and recall one of them and fail. So as usual he was the life of the party, entertaining everyone in the restaurant. Men seem to be drawn to him, he makes a lot of mates. A real man's man. The girls danced, the men listened to his jokes. They tried to match him. They couldn't. No one ever can.

We returned to the house for more drinks. By this time everyone had had more than enough alcohol but that didn't stop any of us. George came out of the bathroom with an entire toilet roll wrapped around him, to everyone's amusement. The jokes flowed again. The men had a singalong of football songs. At one point, George stuck his head through Lauren's legs and tried to lift her off the floor with her dress around his ears, bobbing his head up and down in between her legs. She was not amused. Unfortunately, everyone else was. It *was* funny to watch. It had been a great night with lots of laughs. In our drunken stupor, George drove Kim back to her hotel and us to ours. How he found his way through the maze I don't know. How we arrived safely, I don't know either.

We parked our car and were heading up the stairs to our hotel when we heard some cool music coming from an Irish pub across the way.

"Baileys?" we asked each other. Like we needed more alcohol!

The pub was pumping. It was about three in the morning. We ordered a Baileys on ice each and settled on stools at the bar. The band were great, playing a mix of traditional Irish tunes and pop music. A couple of men appeared beside us. They were giants, about seven foot tall and massively built. I'd not seen anyone that huge before. They looked like giant rugby players. Please don't look at them George, I thought to myself. They looked like trouble. I took myself off to the ladies. I returned to find George with one of them in a headlock, the other one doubled over in laughter! This man has no fear! Wherever we go, people are just drawn to him. He kept them entertained in conversation. They bought us more Bailey's.

I was left sitting on my own while George engaged in joke telling with his new found Icelandic friends. Were they all giants in Iceland I wondered? Two men had noticed I was alone - so they thought - and started chatting me up. Both Irish, I could barely understand a word they were saying. As it turned out, they had lived in Australia for a while and knew the Mercantile pub in Sydney's Rocks area, where my cousin once played in a band. An Irish band funnily enough. So the more they chatted, the closer they got to me until the only thing separating me from one of them was his beer belly. George had been watching this scene unfold from the other side of the bar, finding it hilarious. Wondering how I would handle them, he said. He finally came to my rescue when he saw that one of them was getting a bit 'fresh' with me. They apologised to him and bought us more drinks. More Bailey's.

The band took a break. George took the microphone and told a few jokes. More Bailey's. By the time we left, we'd had six Bailey's each and had only paid for the first round. We staggered back to our hotel at five in the morning. We were meant to meet up with Lauren and Kim for lunch. That didn't happen. We slept till one and headed back to Calpe to sweat out the alcohol.

Kim wanted to visit us in Calpe for a few days. She was going to book herself into a hotel. "Don't be silly, there's more than enough room in Angie's flat for you" I told her. "Save your money and stay with us". I checked that this was okay with George, that he wouldn't feel put out that my friend was staying. Of course he was fine. So Kim hired herself a car and drove up and stayed in Calpe. She was another independent woman happy to travel on her own. We were happy to show her the town, it felt like home to us and we loved it. Much nicer than where she'd just been in Torrevieja, it is very flat and monotonous along that part of the Spanish coast. Calpe is surrounded by mountains and even some of the coastal villages nearby are steep to get down to. It is very scenic with a lovely old town section just up the hill from our flat.

She slept on a sofa bed in the lounge room. Her first night, George was up to his usual pranks. Bouncing up and down on our bed, making the springs squeak and screaming "*Oh* Judi. Yes, oh, oh, *oh yes!*" as she tried to sleep. Ever the fool. We lazed on the beach during the days - I kept my top on while she was there. Girlfriends are funny aren't they? I had no problem going topless around total strangers, but not with my own friends. Took her to Sinatra's bar the first night, she was hit on by not one, but three men. Those Spaniards.

We drove into Benidorm on the second night. I really wanted her to see this party town. I knew she'd love it. We had a brilliant night. The comedian's were on top form. We took her to see the famous 'magic' act from the woman in her sixties - she was gob-smacked as well. We ended up in the same bar where George had proposed to me twelve months previously. He was in a better mood this night. Kim and I purchased some cocktails in giant colourful penis bottles with a straw stuck in the hole at the top. We took lots of photos and had a huge laugh. She was happy to see me so happy.

On her third night with us, Calpe was celebrating the start of a three day festival - the 'Moors and Christians' fiesta. There was to be a parade through the main street, just behind our flat. We settled ourselves into a good position and watched the start of the parade. It was spectacular. Decorated floats of all designs, groups of warriors in medieval costumes, dance groups, drummers, marching bands all marched down the Calle. We watched for over an hour then decided to have some dinner. We headed off to a Chinese restaurant we'd discovered and enjoyed a leisurely meal. Included in the set price was a bottle of wine and a bottle of peach schnapps! Expecting that the parade would be well and truly over when we left, to our amazement it was still in full swing! How could there be that many people in it, that it was still going three hours after it started? It was the most incredible festival I had ever witnessed.

We said our goodbyes to Kim the next day, she was heading off to Barcelona, on her own. It was emotional, we didn't know when we would see each other again. I had no idea how long I would be away, or if I was ever to come home to live again.

To our astonishment, the parade started up again the next night, and the next. It was loud and the people partied till the early hours of each morning. On the final afternoon before the last children's parade, they had a re-enactment of the Christians arriving by sea to rid the Moors from the lands. I think that's how the legend went. Complete with cannon fire, this performance lasted for an hour with the loudest explosions deafening everyone around. I was surprised it wasn't breaking the windows of the beachfront hotels. We were very fortunate to have been witness to this three day event. Angie had never had the good fortune of seeing it. She didn't even know about it.

The following weekend, it started raining Friday night. 'The rain in Spain falls mainly on the plain' so the saying goes - and on the coastal villages. It didn't stop till Saturday afternoon. I mean, didn't stop *at* all. No break in between downpours, no easing off, just continuous heavy rain for eighteen hours. It had a devastating effect on Calpe. The dry river bed down the hill from our flat had been dry for so many years it had grass and gardens growing in it. It became a raging torrent rushing into the sea. Buildings either side of the streets along side it and side streets running off these roads were under a metre of water. Every business and bar was ruined, including our own Sinatra's. Underground car parks became swimming pools with cars piled on top of one another. Cars parked in the streets floated by and crashed into each other. The road where the torrent raged under on its rush to the sea, just broke up and washed onto the beach. The beautiful promenade was ruined, the two foot high wall that lined the edge gone, in places. Just fallen off the edge. There were some really dangerous sections where parts of the promenade had broken off and there was nothing underneath to stop more falling into the sea. Incredibly it was to be three days before any of it was roped off from the public. It was amazing no one was hurt from it.

We discovered all this devastation when we finally ventured out of the flat after the rain stopped. People wandered around totally despondent. So did we. It was heart wrenching seeing the damage. It had even appeared on the news in Australia, it was so bad. My daughters had seen it. Every business was shut down for months while they cleaned up and repaired the damage. We wondered if any of them would be gone forever. We were lucky, we were flying to Cyprus the next day. We would have helped with the clean up if we had stayed.

So we said goodbye to our beautiful Calpe.

Chapter 16

Red Red Wine

Stage four of our adventure began. We flew into Paphos, Cyprus on a thing called a charter flight. There were six passengers and four crew on board. We sat where we wanted on the plane, able to stretch out across three seats and have a sleep.

George had booked an apartment for us to stay in for two weeks while we had a good look around. The apartment was everything it appeared on the internet - modern, well furnished, large balcony, lovely tropical gardens and a beautiful pool with sunbeds. What it hadn't shown in the photos of course was that it was on the main dual carriageway in and out of the city. The noise was deafening, and constant. He was really ticked off. I calmed him down, it wasn't worth getting stressed over - we'd paid the money, they weren't about to refund it, I assured him.

"You're always so calm and logical about things, that's what I love about you" he told me. You haven't seen me when things go wrong at home, I thought to myself.

I really enjoyed Paphos. The longer I stayed and got to know it, the more it grew on me. We hired a car for a month, just a bombey old thing but it was cheap and it did the job. We explored little bays and coves, found some lovely beaches and villages and drove up into the surrounding mountains and enjoyed spectacular views to the sea. George was anxious to see if I liked it enough to live there. I did, it was growing on me.

The main entertainment area was an easy walk from the apartment, so we hardly ever drove into it. All the main bars and restaurants were located on one street known as 'Bar Street' so we soon became regulars. We found a bar that became our home base - it was run by an Australian Cypriot, with another Aussie Cypriot as the head barman. Phil took me under his wing, as it was really rare to find an Aussie over there. Every time he made a cocktail for someone (they were his specialty), he gave me the leftovers. It was nothing for me to have consumed around six full cocktails in a session, all in small doses.

Cyprus was an incredibly safe place to be. Hardly any crime, it was heartening to see the sea-front area heaving with people of a night, young groups intermingled with oldies, all getting along fine with each other. No agro anywhere. I was impressed.

It was so safe, that on many nights Phil and the other barman would take their dinner breaks together and disappear for half an hour up the street. Leaving the bar open with sometimes up to eight or so customers in it, not concerned at all about theft. George would jokingly tell them that where he came from in Yorkshire, if that happened not only would the alcohol have disappeared, but all the fixtures and fittings as well.

We had lots of laughs and as usual, attracted lots of attention. There were many funny moments, I remembered one night walking down to Bar Street and I was wearing those stay up stockings with the lacy tops and sticky elastic to hold them up. George loved me in stockings - the things we do to please a man. Well, by the time we arrived at the bar, they were down around my ankles. They would not stay up. In the end I had to take them off, George wore them as a tie around his neck.

We started looking for a place to rent. Prices were pretty reasonable and we saw some nice flats. We happened upon a really lovely house about ten miles away in a place called Coral Bay. It was a little out of town along a narrow winding road but we fell in love with it. It had a swimming pool and came fully furnished, with air conditioning. The real estate agent was really giving us the hard sell, dropping the price if we agreed to it today. Against my better judgement, I found myself handing over one hundred pounds deposit (quite a lot of money - their currency was very strong at the time). George was useless, he was such a softie when it came to negotiating.

As soon as we did it and drove off, we regretted it. It was too far away from where we wanted to be, and George would never have found it in the dark if we'd been out for the evening. It was down a goat track and quite isolated. We rang her and cancelled the deal. We didn't get our deposit back.

During one of our nights down at the bar, we met Dennis. Dennis had a holiday villa to rent five minutes walk away, he liked us so said we could have it at a very nominal rent for as long as we needed it. So that was that sorted. We moved into it at the end of the two weeks at the other flat.

I found a local hairdressers nearby. I was in desperate need of a cut and colour. They didn't speak English, but it was very trendy so I thought I would be safe. Just wanting a trim, I went in with blonde curly hair and came out with dark brown straight hair! When I walked in to home, George was cooking dinner. Before he could launch into a barrage of jokes, I gave him 'the look' that warned him to keep his mouth shut. You know that look? The one that tells a man its not worth losing his manhood over? I took myself straight upstairs and washed it out. Dried it to some sort of semblance to how it was. George put blonde foils back in it the following day.

The usual thing happened - everywhere we went we made friends easily. We both loved chatting to people and we became a bit of a novelty item - me from Australia with this clown who entertained everyone. We became regulars at every quiz night we could find. A couple of the quiz masters took their roles way too serious, and didn't appreciate George's banter and quick wit, so we didn't go back. They were supposed to be fun, weren't they?

At one of these quiz nights we took our seats in a large crowded pub and suddenly George swapped seats with me, placing his back to the crowd. He'd just spotted his wife's best friend and her husband

and another guy he knew. He couldn't let them see him there - with me. Jane didn't know where he was, nor who he was with. And he didn't want her knowing. She'd been giving him a hard time of their break up. So the night was rather dull - he couldn't call out funny answers and play up like he usually did. He just had to sit there with me keeping watch to see if they were looking. He couldn't even go to the toilet. When the quiz was over, we had to wait till they left before he could make a move. When they finally did get up to leave, one of them called over his shoulder "Goodnight George". Oh god, they had seen him.

He became really concerned. He knew they'd message Jane straight away to tell her. He knew she'd know who the blonde woman was. He was in trouble. She'd already agreed to a divorce, now knowing it was me she would retract it. She would never agree to it now, just to spite him. At the same time, he'd also been trying to contact his daughter. He doted on her, spoilt her way more than I thought was healthy. None of my business though, I said nothing. When he finally got hold of her, she abused him for what he'd done. Jane had contacted her, crying on her shoulder. Things were a mess. He couldn't bear his daughter not talking to him. She told him she would never agree to meet me, didn't want to know me.

This stress caused a lot of tension for both of us. I cried on his shoulder when he told me what his daughter had said. "She's never even met me and I've become the enemy. This is so unfair, I've been hung, drawn and quartered and I haven't done anything" I sobbed to him. I had so been wanting to meet her, she was the same age as my eldest daughter. I had hoped we could all be one happy family one day. That was not going to happen. I was miserable, but George was worse. He finally rang Jane one day after he'd been to have a haircut. Without me in tow. He tried to smooth things over with her. This isn't how he wanted her to find out about me. He had wanted to sit down with her and explain everything. Her friends beat him to it.

His behaviour started to change ever so slightly. Nothing bad, just little things he'd say to me. I remember emailing Angie who was having some problems with her new man, and telling her it was no bed of roses for me either sometimes. 'Maybe we've just been on our own too long' I would say to her, 'it's not easy learning to live with someone again.' I thought that was all it was - an adjustment time.

George had managed to get a little work, just an odd day here and there. The pay was terrible, a fraction of what he would get back in the UK.

We were still having a great time though. He'd joined the local darts team, and we'd met a couple on their holidays and went to dinner with them a few times. Had a couple of golf days with them. I didn't play golf, so I drove the buggy. We had a lovely time with them.

His behaviour was getting more irritating to me. He would make me the brunt of his jokes, making fun of some of the things I would say to people that were different to the English way. I didn't mind being made fun of, but when it went on way past being funny, it was a bit tiresome. He also started swearing a lot more, he knew I disliked it. It was like he was deliberately trying to turn me off him.

I also starting seeing sides of him I didn't know he had. A jealous streak for one. We were out one night with the regulars from the bar and his darts mates and wandered up to a dance club. Phil had introduced us to a mate of his who was over here on his own and asked if we could let him tag along. No problems for us. We chatted away, he was interested in investment property so we had a bit in common. I chatted to him like I would with anyone who was alone, just being friendly. George had been talking to another group of people so it was just the two of us, talking at the bar. George went off to the toilet, and never came back to me. Just disappeared. Left me there with all the men - I was the only female. Half an hour went by, they were getting worried. He's probably just gone out for some fresh air, I told them. They looked for him. He was nowhere to be found. Some of them got really angry at him. "You don't just leave your woman at a bar with all men and piss off" they were saying. One of them offered to take me home on his bike. I didn't have the keys to the flat, George did. I was feeling really embarrassed by this stage. I said I'd go looking for him and left, with instructions to come back to them if I couldn't find him. They were nice guys.

I finally found him down at the internet café we used. We had our first fight. "How dare you leave me with all those men and just piss off!" I yelled at him. "What the hell was that about?" I was livid. He'd never seen me angry before.

"I was jealous of you talking to that guy. I thought you fancied him" he replied.

On another occasion, we'd got home really late and pretty drunk. It seemed like all we did was get drunk, but there wasn't much else to do with neither of us working. He flopped onto the lounge apparently feeling frisky. I didn't know this. I took myself off to the bathroom to wash my make up off and get changed. When I came back to him he was angry at me because I hadn't responded to his friskiness. How was I to know he was horny? He hadn't exactly done anything to show me. Usually after a drinking night it was the last thing he was capable of. So he picked a fight with me, slept on the lounge and declared that he was leaving in the morning. He couldn't do this anymore, he was catching the next flight out of there. Nice one, I thought.

He didn't, of course. He finally came back to bed, apologised to me for his behaviour, said he'd had too much to drink and we kissed and made up.

But the strain was beginning to show. He was running out of money. This holiday had cost him a fortune, I knew that. He'd paid for all of London and the Jamaica trip. He was disillusioned with his job prospects in Cyprus, there was no money to be made here. I felt for him, he really wanted to live here, it was a great place. We had a talk and decided that we would spend Christmas together, then both go back to our respective lands and work to save up some more money for three months, then meet up again in England to settle down. This was early November.

He needed to see his daughter, to win her over, she was still not happy with him. He couldn't bare it. Would I mind if he went to Dubai for a week? No, I thought it was a good idea I told him. I knew how much she meant to him, she was his princess. I couldn't handle it if one of my girls wasn't talking to me either.

So plans were made. We both knew we couldn't stay in Cyprus. We asked Angie if we could use her flat in Calpe again for three weeks in December so we could spend Christmas together before I went home. She was fine with this. The week he would be in Dubai, I was able to stay in an apartment in Nice. I had booked it prior to knowing about my holiday with George and the owner still held my deposit. It was available the week I needed, so it worked out well. We would then meet up in London and fly back down to Calpe to spend those three weeks together.

Things seemed to settle down, we had two weeks left in Cyprus. George still had his moments though. I pinpointed it down to when he'd been drinking red wine - it made him depressed and he would say really dark things. It dawned on me this is what had happened that night in Benidorm a year before when his mood changed - just before he asked me to marry him. He'd been drinking red wine at the end of that night too.

It happened again one night before we left. We'd been bowling, it was the only sport that I was actually better than him at, so I enjoyed it. We'd had a bottle of red wine with dinner before we went, then more while we were there. He got really sulky because I beat him (what a child I thought to myself, it's only a game), and out in the street he plunged into a black hole of depression. About his bad sportsmanship.

"You're the only woman in the world who still loves me, and now I've pissed you off as well" he wailed to me. "Everybody hates me, and now you do too" he continued.

Oh please, do me a favour! Tiresome creatures aren't they, I thought to myself.

We had a final dinner with our golfing friends on our second last night. George was up to his old tricks again, donning a colourful Jamaican beanie with attached dreadlocks in the restaurant and speaking 'Jamaican' lingo. Again, the life of the party.

On our final night, he had to attend the dart's final, he couldn't let them down. He was their best player. I went to dinner with our friends and we all met back at 'our' bar to say our farewells. We of course were telling everyone we would be back, but we knew we wouldn't come back to Cyprus to live. No work there for us. We were in good spirits, George kissing me and hugging me and telling his usual jokes to everyone.

We arrived back at the flat quite late. I made us a cup of tea. We would leave the packing till the morning, we had a bit of time before our flight to London. We sat on the lounge together. I'd stripped off my dress, I was wearing a sexy black teddy and suspenders and stockings for our last night in Cyprus. There was a bit of an un-easy moment when George said something to me. I thought for a moment.

"You're not coming back to me are you?" I asked him. "We're not going to see each other again are we?" I continued.

"No" he said simply. "I'm staying in Dubai" Heartbreak number four. Or was it five, I'd lost count.

Surprisingly, I didn't fall apart. I cried a little, asked him when he had planned on letting me know. "When we got to London tomorrow" he answered guiltily.

Probably never, based on his previous form, I thought to myself.

We stayed seated on the lounge, he stroked my legs and we finished our tea. We discussed a few things. "Come up to bed", I told him, "its late."

"Let's be amicable about this, there's no need for us to be enemies over it" I went on.

God, I've got to stop this being calm and sensible all the time! Why couldn't I scream and shout like most women would have? Damn all that yoga!

I had to be honest with myself. Over the last few weeks, I did start questioning whether this was what I really wanted in my life. I loved this man with all my heart, but he was hard work. I likened him to a spoilt child, used to getting things his own way. With everything. It was his way or not at all. I had been getting these gut churning feelings in my stomach that this wasn't right for me. We should never ignore our instincts, I reminded myself.

We were very civilized to each other the next day. He left me to pack up my suitcase, then he did his. We had bought a new one for him by this stage. We had kept the slide out handle of the broken bag. There was a very funny skit we'd seen a Welsh comedian perform about ending up with just the handle of his suitcase on the luggage carousel. It was very clever, I'd suggested George keep it for a prop and work it into his act.

Dennis drove us to the airport. We left some food items for him, and a cooler bag we'd bought while we were there. Met up with our golfing friends again at the airport - they were heading home as well. We didn't let on that we were splitting up. What was the point, it would just sadden them.

We had booked into a bed and breakfast near Gatwick airport for that night as we weren't continuing our journeys till the following day. So it was strange, here we were about to part and still spent the night together. We had a nice meal out, he still stroked my hair and held my hand as we walked. We had the best sex we'd had in a long time - angry sex if there is such a thing. Break up sex. It was lovely.

He came with me to the airport, but he was flying out of Heathrow. While I waited in line for check in, he decided he'd go and get his coach ticket and check the transfer times. I honestly didn't expect to see him again. I thought he'd make his escape to avoid saying goodbye. To my surprise he did come back to me, and just as well. I was really upset - my camera was missing out of my handbag. The little case was still there, just the camera was missing. I must have left it in the bar or restaurant the night before. It couldn't have been stolen, they would have taken it in its case. We were both really upset over it - I think the stress had got to us both. Luckily, I'd changed the memory card just the week before as the previous one was full. It had all the photos of the entire nine weeks on it. I was so relieved. This memory card only had the last weeks photos, and I knew I would be able to ask our golf friends to send me theirs.

It was time to say goodbye. We hugged each other for a long time. I thanked him for a wonderful holiday, one I certainly would never forget. He said the same. We kissed one last time and I was on my way. I didn't cry this time. I was just numb.

Chapter 17

Lost in Nice

My flight to Nice was one of mixed emotions. I was incredibly sad at what had just happened, but somehow knew it was going to. The universe working its weird ways again. I believe I have guardian angels that look out for me, and somehow they knew this wasn't the right thing for me. So they ended it in the least painful way they could.

After collecting the keys to my little pied-a-terre in the old town of Nice and settling in, there was something I really had to do. I rang my daughters to tell them. They were really shocked and sad for me. And surprised that I was not falling apart. Nicole was wonderful, I expected her to want me on the first flight home, but she suggested I stay over there a while longer to get my head together. Not much was happening work wise, I might as well enjoy Europe while I'm there.

I emailed Angie and told her I wouldn't be needing her flat. Again, she was shocked at my news. I had an email that night from my friend Di who didn't know anything about it. "Are you okay? I had a dream that something bad was happening to you and my cards have told me the same thing" her email read. "Let me know if you're okay" she said. Di is quite psychic and reads her own tarot cards. A 'white witch' I've heard some call her, I just call her a witch sometimes. Times like these. She'd picked it.

My second day in Nice I decided I should report my camera missing. That way I could at least make a claim against my travel insurance. I bought a replacement camera on my way to the police station though. I didn't want to be without a camera, there was still plenty to photograph. I loved Nice, it's one of my favourite places. I was interviewed by a charming, handsome French police officer. Yes, even in my heartbroken state I still recognised a good looking man when I saw one. He completed the paper work. In his broken English he asked me if I was sure that was all that was missing.

"Are you absolutely certain that is all that has been stolen madame? No money, no personal items? You must carry more valuables in your handbag, surely" he prompted.

"No, just the camera is gone" I insisted.

At the end of the interview he then asked me if I would like to join him for 'une café' sometime! I'd already noticed the ring on his finger. "Merci monsieur, mais non" I replied. I wasn't going down that path again.

Only when I was walking back from there did I realize what he was implying with his questioning. He was prompting me to add more things to claim as stolen. Even if they weren't. How dumb was I? Then I remembered the ring. I decided I would return the next day and report it missing as well. Give them a story that I'd only just discovered it gone. It was only half a white lie, I told myself. It had been stolen after all, just not on the same occasion. Might as well get some of my money back for it, I thought.

The temperatures were getting quite cool of an evening, it was now the start of December. I would wander around the city during the day, moping mostly and wondering what the hell had just happened to me. But I was surprised at how well I was taking it, actually. Nothing like the last time. Or was I just getting used to it? I wasn't ready to go home just yet. Couldn't face anyone. So I extended my stay in the little flat for another week, then decided to have another couple of days in London before heading home for Christmas. A Christmas without George. That was what was hurting the most, that I would not get to have Christmas with him, again. That's what I had always wanted. It wasn't ever going to happen.

The days dragged on, I did sight-seeing by day and kept to myself at night, staying indoors as it was now too cold to be out. At some stage I must have had a turning point - no more moping I told myself. Get yourself dolled up and get down to the Casino. Find yourself a rich man to mend your heart, my inner person was telling me.

So, reflecting on a completely immoral French film I'd seen with Angie that year, I decided I'd go and see what I could attract. An Audrey Tautou film called 'Priceless', she hung about posh hotels conning rich men into paying for her meals then worming her way into their hearts and getting them to pay her way. She made a living out of gold-digging. It was a very funny movie, set exactly where I was at the moment, in Nice and Monaco.

If it's good enough for Audrey Tautou, it's good enough for me I decided.

Of course it didn't work. Who was I kidding? The last thing I needed right now was another man to do my head in. My heart was still battered and bruised, a bit like my head had been a few weeks earlier. I needed time to heal. I played the poker machines for a while, kept my head down and prayed those pheromones had stopped working.

They had, to a point. I did get chatted up in McDonalds one day - I was craving for some junk food. Or anything that wasn't French. As usual, a rude dumpy little French man had pushed in ahead of me where I had been politely queuing, and I gave him a piece of my mind. An English man a few people behind me obviously liked my feistiness. He took me for tea and scones in a lovely tea parlour. Still living with his parents back in England, he came to the south of France for summers to aid his skin condition. Oh dear, here's a catch I thought.

Finding a flight home this close to Christmas proved more difficult than I imagined. After much too-ing and fro-ing, I finally was able to change my flight to leave on the 16th. At considerably more cost. I would be home for my birthday. Oh joy. I left the flat in Nice a few days earlier than I'd arranged with the owner. I really wanted a couple of days in London before I left. Who knew when I'd be back again, I wondered.

I spent the day at Hampton Court Palace when I arrived back in London. It was a wonderful day. Got lost in the maze and took twenty minutes to find my way out of the bloody thing. Bitterly cold at just seven degrees, I was thankful I had brought my red overcoat with me on this trip. I loved this coat, again I called it my 'Paris' coat as I only ever used it when I went to Paris. Never cold enough back home for it. I wrapped a pashmina around my head to keep the cold out, donned my gloves and enjoyed the winter sunshine.

I took myself off to see 'Wicked' at the theatre. I ended up leaving at interval. I didn't enjoy it, something about the story of a person being ostracized for being different just rubbed me the wrong way. I'm sure it was that I was in a bad (sad) place at the time was more likely the reasoning. I filled in the second day around Oxford Street, purchasing a few bits and pieces to take home to my girls.

By the time departure day arrived, I was glad to be going home. Where I belonged. Where my family and friends were. Where I was missed.

Chapter 18

Blackouts

Everyone was happy to see me, especially my daughters. My friends were delighted I was back home. Of course they were sad for me, but were incredibly relieved to see me taking it so well. I'm fairly certain there were a few cynics among them who expected I would come home with my tail between my legs, completely humiliated that it hadn't worked out with George again. I held my head high. I had just had the most incredible experience with this man and had amazing memories of it. Why should I be humiliated? At least we ended it before it caused more heartache.

I was reminded of a line in an email someone once sent me:

"Don't cry because it is over, smile because it happened."

Even my ex-husband was happy to see me. "Glad your back, back home where you belong" he'd said to me when I arrived back at Nicole's. I expected a lecture from him, an 'I told you so'.

Instead he just said "Oh well, another chapter of your life closed. Move onto the next one". He was mellowing in his old age.

He was recuperating from major heart surgery at her house, he looked surprisingly well considering it had only been three weeks. Went in for a stent, came out with a quadruple bypass. The following day I took him with me to my investment house. The tenant had contacted Nicole to say the pool filter wasn't working well. My ex knew a thing or two about pools - we'd had one at our home - so offered to try and fix it before I called the professionals out. I got a fit of the giggles when he was arm deep in the skimmer box.

"How absurd is this" I started "I'm here at my *ex* lover's old house with my *ex* husband doing maintenance for me" I explained through the laughter. Yes, he did see the irony in the situation.

I was very displaced over the next two months. I had no home to go back to after selling my town house, and my belongings were locked in storage. I house sat Angie's house for six weeks while she was in England, then moved into my hairdresser's home for a month to house sit for her. By the end of February I finally moved into an apartment of my own. With my own belongings surrounding me, I slowly started feeling settled again. It was a beautiful apartment, brand new and overlooking a marina. I finally had a proper office and bought myself a beautiful white timber and glass desk and white leather chair to work from. I was able to gaze out of the window to the canal while I worked. It was very stimulating for me. The complex had two fabulous pools and a gym to exercise in. I was very comfortable.

I thought it sensible to get my head checked out after that bump to it, while I house sat. I had an x-ray and a scan and thankfully there was no damage. I had a thick skull obviously. However, when I moved into my apartment, I started having blackouts. Not dizzy spells, actual blackouts. For a couple of seconds. I would actually have to grab hold of something until I 'came back'. They were happening around six times a day. At the same time, my jaw locked. I couldn't open my mouth to eat. I took myself off to my osteopath for my jaw and mentioned the blackouts. My jaw was out because of the bump to my head, even though it was on the opposite side of my head, he concluded. The force of the knock had shifted my entire jaw line. When he fixed my jaw, the blackouts stopped! It was absurd, but this mis-alignment of my jaw was pressing on a nerve to my brain and shutting it down for a second. I'd been lucky.

George and I had exchanged a couple of brief emails in the days after we parted, just keeping it pleasant really. Saying we'd keep in touch with other, take care, etc, etc. I let him know I'd arrived home safely as requested. I knew I wouldn't hear from him after that for a while. I gave him three months before I expected any contact from him again. I even made bets with my friends for the end of March. I just knew how he worked. True to form, an email popped into my inbox on the second of April. I was two days out with my prediction! I knew him well.

"dearest judi ,hope you are keeping well. Im always thinking of you ,hope to meet again one day as you are one of the best women Ive ever met. Be good xxxxxx"

That was all I got. His typing skills hadn't improved, I noticed.

"Is that it? How about some news about what you've been up to? Where you're working now? What mischief you've been up to? etc, etc....... PS - glad to hear from you. Keep in touch xxxxxx" was my response.

I did get a reply explaining what he was up to. Still in Dubai but not sure for how much longer, on good terms with his daughter again, what are my plans now, that kind of thing. We kept the emails going with light hearted banter.

"By the way, I have a bone of contention with you about that first email" I replied.

" I've now been relegated to 'one of the best women you ever met?' Huh, a year ago I was *the* best woman you'd ever met! Sounds like I've got some competition now hey?" I continued in my email.

"I stand corrected" was his reply. "And no, you don't have any competition, believe me".

Emails continued between each other as the months went by. Light hearted, nothing heavy. Although one night after I'd been out for my usual Friday night with the girls, I sent an 'I'm bored' email.

"I had an overwhelming emotional sensation yesterday morning when I was driving that I want to tell you about. (Its a wonder you didn't sense something, it was that strong.) The song 'love is in the air' came on the radio and I had wonderful memories of you singing it in the piano bar in Jamaica to me and me feeling so proud of your talents and I was remembering how madly in love I was with you then. And all I could think was - fuck you george wilkinson - I miss you so much and I miss what we had and I never stop wishing we could have it all over again. So there, I've said it, and I've used the 'f' word and I'll probably regret sending this email to you in the morning, but after three glasses of red wine I don't care! And don't they say you usually say what's on your mind when your drunk? So there. I know I'll probably scare you off for another month or so but that's okay.

I still love you heaps you know and yes, fuck you for that. There, I said it again…."

He loved that email. Yes, he still loved me too and missed me every day. Yes, he realized now what we had was love and not a fly by night thing and he hoped we could meet up again one day, sooner rather than later. Went on with some other stuff about what he'd like to do if he did see me again - he was such a romantic!

" behave yourself and keep it in yor knickers" he finished off with.

Chapter 19

French Champagne, Madam?

Business waxed and waned with the moon it seemed. Some months were great, others nothing happened. I still made a reasonable living though. Nicole had had a good year also and was itching for another holiday. Her partner was not a traveller, so would I like to do a tour of the UK with her? I'd raved about London to her since I'd been. Never one to knock back the prospect of a holiday, of course I agreed. We planned for a short break of just two weeks this time - it was too difficult for us both to be away from the business together. We booked a tour of England, Scotland and Wales at a very reasonable price. For September again. I always seemed to be away for my sisters' birthdays. I was always phoning them from some exotic place on the other side of the world. Under the Eiffel Tower one year, the piazza in Sienna another.

We were thrilled to discover that my uncle and his son were arriving in London from Paris on the same afternoon that our tour finished. Uncle Brian was now eighty three and had never travelled. He had a fascination with Egyptology and there was nothing he didn't know about it. My cousin was taking him on a five week tour. So I was delighted that he would actually get to see these lands that he'd studied like a religion. We would meet up with them for dinner in London and accompany them to the Tower of London the next day. He had moved into a retirement home in Melbourne near his son after the house in Sydney sold. I was happy for that.

George was actually going to be in England just as we arrived. We wanted to catch up. After emailing backwards and forwards we worked out that the only time we could do it was the night I arrived. I had planned out an itinerary for me and Nicole for that first day as we arrived very early in the morning. She would be exhausted by dinner time as she never sleeps on planes. So she was happy (sort of) for me to go to dinner with George and stay with him that night. It was easier for him to book into the same hotel, which was where our tour commenced from. I knew it would be chaotic in the morning as our tour group boarded the coach, so it made sense for him to stay there.

I played tour guide with Nicole on our first day in London. Oh, how I loved this city. So vibrant and bustling, it was great to see it again. A ride on the London Eye, a river cruise, the tour through Buckingham Palace - again, it was open until the end of September. Oxford and Regent Streets on a red bus. We had a full day and she was grateful for a peaceful night to herself.

I showered, changed and freshened up and made my way up to George's room at the designated time. He answered the door in nothing but a towel, still dripping wet.

"Wanted to dispense with the formalities, did you" I laughed. "straight down to business is it?"

It was lovely to see each other again. We hugged and kissed, drank champagne and joked about each other's bellies that had grown since our last encounter. A new round of jokes for me, he'd added to his repertoire. He whipped off his towel in matador style. We made love for an hour. It was just like old times. We'd missed each other. We were still in love with each other.

We had a wonderful night, as always. Dinner in his favourite Korean restaurant, another comedy club for an hour, a walk along Carnaby Street and a couple of pubs along the way for a few nightcaps. And back to the hotel to bed. The jet lag had set in.

I had no recollection afterwards of getting back to the hotel, let alone getting into bed. I must have gone out like a light when my head hit the pillow.

"Did you have your wicked way with me?" I asked George the next morning.

"Nah, I'm sure I'd remember that" I joked. He was a great lover, I wouldn't have slept through that I'm sure.

"No, I did not. You were out cold. I don't do cadavers. And you still snore" he joked back.
Oh dear. How embarrassing.

Nicole joined us for breakfast. I was grateful to her that she was very gracious to George, chatting to him about the tour and showing him her new I-phone. I knew how she felt about him and what he'd done to me - rather, what he *kept* doing to me.

It was time for us to board our coach. Nicole took charge of getting our cases on board while I said my goodbyes to George with promises to each other to stay in touch.

Our tour was fabulous. I thoroughly enjoyed it. We had both been a little hesitant when we booked it. We both had this ill conceived idea that coach tours were full of grey haired old ladies who had long retired and fobbed off their husbands to either their graves or a nursing home. How wrong we were! Holidays with my daughters up till now had always been a driving tour with me as the designated driver not seeing much more than the dividing line in the road. But because of the history throughout the UK, I wanted a tour guide. So this was a breath of fresh air.

A mixed range of ages, Nicole was thrilled to note that there were quite a few in her own age group. Many were in mine and only a few were a little older. Our tour guide was a walking history book - she knew everything about everywhere. She was brilliant. And so well prepared - she had it down to a fine art. As we entered different regions, she had music appropriate for that area. Beautiful traditional Scottish songs, Welsh choirs, 'The Green Green Grass of Home' as we passed through Tom Jones territory.

We learnt so much from this tour, so much we hadn't a clue about. The battle of Culloden, where we stopped to walk the battlefields. Our guide went on to tell us about a series of books based loosely around this last Jacobite uprising. The story sounded so fascinating about stone circles and time travel and

Highland warriors that Nicole bought the series when she returned home and read them all. I did the same a year later when I had the time to read. Once I started I couldn't put them down, and went on to lend them out to my friends. We'd started our own book club of sorts. Just from that one fascinating story from Scotland.

As with any large group of people, there would always be one person that was a 'bit of a problem'. That person was Bruce. He was travelling alone and Bruce was a little 'slow'. He was always last back on the bus, he'd go off on his own - as we all could do - but he had no sense of direction and would lose his bearings. Nor did he wear a watch. So much of our time was spent in search of Bruce. It did bring out the best in people though, we all as a group developed a mother hen attitude to him. One day he had to get our driver to make a toilet stop on the side of the road. He disappeared down a gully and behind the woods for privacy. One of the girls saw him in the rear view mirror and leapt out of her seat and raced down to him, taking some of the men with her. Poor Bruce couldn't get back up the gully and kept falling back down to the bottom. He had been grabbing hold of poison ivy to pull himself up the hill and ended up with the most awful rash and stinging hands. And a severe case of embarrassment. Poor love. He made a lot of friends on that tour.

It was one of the best holidays I'd had, not counting the one's with George. Nothing could beat those for sheer fun and laughter. But this was so stress free. The only thing I had to worry about was having my suitcase outside my door by seven each morning. Not even every morning, there were many places we stayed two nights. It was so much better than we had hoped for.

And so began a love affair with Britain. I couldn't get enough of it.

We met up with my cousin and uncle as arranged and enjoyed a beautiful dinner in their hotel. Complete with a very expensive bottle of Chateauneuf du Pape wine, compliments of my now very financially comfortable uncle. Nicole and I particularly enjoyed it, we had stayed in the Rhone region in France some years before, but certainly couldn't include that luxury in our holiday budget.

A tour of the Tower of London followed the next day. It was so lovely and somewhat surreal to meet up with family from home all the way over here in London. We were delighted that we had the opportunity to share this with Brian, I knew it would be his one and only grand tour. Wish I'd been able to share it with Joyce also.

Nicole and I did hire a car for a few days to cover some places that we still wanted to see. I wanted to show her Brighton, I'd been there the previous year with George and I loved it. Also, I was keen to have a look at some areas further along the coast as I was interested in purchasing a flat somewhere to keep as a base for my European jaunts when I retired. Brighton didn't hold the same appeal to Nicole unfortunately. She was sick with a cold she'd picked up from the tour and it was a grey rainy day so it didn't float her boat. We continued along towards Dover, dropping into seaside towns briefly for me to look at. We wanted to stay in Canterbury that evening to explore the cathedral the next day.

As it was late afternoon by the time we arrived, we first had to start looking for a hotel or bed and breakfast for the night. Everywhere was booked out, there was some event on in Canterbury that weekend. On and on we drove, way past Canterbury in search of a place to stay. No rooms anywhere. We spent the night in a Day's Inn at Dartford Crossing! It was the only room we could find. Not before I'd spent six pound on tolls going back across it three times trying to locate the correct turn off. We could see the hotel's neon sign, just couldn't get to it. A bit like my experience on Sydney's Harbour Bridge. No sat-nav this time though.

When we caught up with our English friend's on our final day, they thought it was hilarious. Dartford Crossing is surrounded by nothing but smoke stacks and factories, it is an industrial district. Probably the most un-touristy place we could have ended up. Quite ugly in the daylight as we discovered. Of all the beautiful places we could have stayed, they said. Of course, we didn't get to see Canterbury Cathedral.

Our holiday was over. Time for the flight home. We had planned a stopover in Abu Dhabi, we had never been before. Our airline stopped there en-route. We had booked into an executive suite at the Hilton hotel and had also booked a desert safari tour for the afternoon. One of those dune bashing, camel riding, barbecue dinners in a Bedouin tent events.

Something completely different, we were so looking forward to it.

Only, the day before departure I had caught Nicole's bug. Not just a cold, full on flu complete with aching bones, fevers, headache, earache, sore throat, runny nose - the whole package. I was so ill I probably shouldn't have flown. I felt like I was going to die on the flight. I just sat, upright, trying to remain calm and breathe slowly the entire flight. All I wanted to do was lie down and sleep, as you do when these flu's hit you. Fortunately, part of this 'executive' booking included free transfers from the airport in a limousine, so I didn't have to struggle with bags and transport in my state.

We were far too early for check-in, our room wasn't ready. They sent us up to the executive floor to wait, until we could move into it. We were ushered into a bar area that had the most beautiful spread of breakfast foods imaginable. All exquisitely presented, a vast selection of both hot and cold foods from many nations, and juices of every flavour. And all I could manage was a half a glass of watermelon juice.

What a terrible waste. I sat on one of the soft leather sofas blowing my nose, wiping my watery eyes and feeling miserable.

"Would you try and look human? You look pathetic. It's embarrassing" my darling daughter hissed at me. A total lack of sympathy, she got that from her father.

"Nicole, I'm really sick. I really need to be in bed. I'm not putting this on" I argued with her. She helped herself to more plates of food. She ate my share as well.

After having a word to the staff at the reception desk and pointing over to me, Nicole persuaded them to allow us early entry into our room.

"See that pathetic looking woman over there? Well, we need to get her out of sight of the other guests" I imagined her telling the receptionist.

I collapsed into bed. Fever number one hit me. Nicole had to draw the curtains, I couldn't stand the light in the room. She left me to sleep for a while and explored the hotel. It was beautiful, very opulent. With a magnificent pool area that lead down to the beach.

She returned to check on me. I was now passing through fever number two. Shaking and sweating, coughing and wheezing. Our desert safari tour was kicking off at three o'clock, it was already nearly lunchtime. It was obvious I was in no fit state to go. You'll have to go alone, I told her. She didn't want to go alone. We had seen another mother and daughter in the foyer earlier that morning, perhaps she could find them and see if the daughter would like to take my place, I suggested. She let me know what she thought of my suggestion. "I'm not going up to a perfect stranger and asking them that!" she half screamed at me. Why not? I would have had no problem doing it.

In the end, I realized she was actually quite concerned about me. She just had a strange way of showing it. We were not a family of mollycoddler's. My fault I guess.

To her credit, she rang the company in Australia that she had booked the tour with, explained the situation to them and they were fantastic. They arranged a complete refund immediately, contacted the tour group to cancel for her and even found her the number of a doctor in Abu Dhabi to call for assistance. We were very impressed with them. She then spoke to the doctor, described all my symptoms to him and he gave her a list of what she needed to purchase from the chemist. What fantastic service.

With directions from the hotel staff, she found her way to a chemist and came back armed with all manner of sprays and tablets and lozenges for me. Once again, with the correct medicines prescribed, I made a rapid recovery. Still not well enough to have been able to go on the safari, it was a seven hour tour. Who would want to ride a camel feeling the way I did, I thought to myself. I felt really sorry for Nicole though. She was missing out on it, but she was okay about it.

Later in the afternoon after I had slept some more, we made our way over to the huge shopping mall. It was gorgeous, they really know how to show off their wealth there. We returned to the executive floor of the hotel to check our emails, and discovered they were serving canapé's and pre dinner drinks. How lovely. My appetite had returned (it never disappears for long, sadly) and I was famished. I hadn't eaten for almost twenty four hours. We stuffed ourselves silly. As politely as one can - we were in the executive lounge after all. Personal waiters in impeccable uniforms served us our drinks.

"Would madam care for some French champagne?" they asked.

Yes, madam would, thank you very much.

By the time we ventured out for dinner, we weren't hungry. It saved us a small fortune. This city is not cheap. So we made our way over to the pool area - curiously you had to walk through an underpass under a busy road to reach it. It was magnificent at night. Palm trees lit with coloured lights, floating candles in the pool, plenty of lively bars and music. And paths that led onto the beach. We enjoyed the rest of our stay, sipping on soda waters. We'd both had too much champagne......

Chapter 20

Dawn Service

Life went back to normal when I returned home. Well normal for me that is. Business picked up. We had a few good sales to keep the wheel's in motion. Emails to and from George continued along in much the same easy manner. No more empty promises being made, just like friends keeping in touch. It was curious, we discussed how each of us only had each other to pour our thoughts out to, vent when things were tough. We were both in the same position in that we were always the upbeat one in our group of friends, always jovial and cheering others up if they were down. No one ever asked us how things were going, if everything was okay in our lives, they just assumed it was because we were always laughing and making others laugh. So we poured out our problems and concerns to each other, via email. It was nice.

George often ended his emails to me with "behave yerself 'n keep it in yor knickers". I would reply:

"If I keep it in my knickers much longer, I'm going to explode!" Strange saying, I thought. I still have no idea what it means!

I did have a run of good fortune though, after a particularly bad run of things going wrong. This new year was going to be my year to shine, I'd convinced myself. And it did start out wonderfully. One day in January I received a phone call while I was out doing viewings with Nicole. It was Emirates airlines rewards department, to inform me I had won two business class tickets to anywhere in the world! I had used my points in some raffle tickets for charity, as they were about to expire. I was the December winner! I'd never won anything this big in my life! I was thrilled. Business class! I had to get her to repeat it, I thought I'd misheard her. How exciting! I had twelve months to use them.

Nicole and I had already planned our next holiday for April - we were to attend the Anzac Day ceremony in Villers-Bretonneux in the Somme Valley in France. My great uncle is buried there, we had visited his gravesite twice before on previous trips to France. Or rather, his name on the wall amongst the 11,000 Australian soldiers whose bodies were never found. The town had celebrated the 90th anniversary the year before with a huge dawn ceremony and had declared it such a success they were to repeat it every year. It was of particular significance to me as my father had been named after this uncle who lost his life to the great war at the age of nineteen.

Nicole had finally convinced her partner to travel, so we all planned a trip around this ceremony. We would spend a few days in Paris after Anzac Day, they would then fly to Canada to begin a fabulous tour and cruise, leaving me to my own devices in Europe. Problem was, we had all booked and paid for the flights for this trip. So I couldn't use my free tickets for that holiday. I would just have to plan another holiday or two to use them. What a problem to have!

There began a dilemma - do I keep them for myself and use them on two separate occasions? Could I afford two more holidays within the twelve months? I doubted it. Would I even want two more holidays within the twelve months? I didn't think so. So I decided to share the tickets with my daughters. Although, I told myself, I'm sure I wouldn't have got a look in if either of them had won them, they wouldn't have given me a thought. The thought did cross my mind to share my prize with George, but my girls would never forgive me if I did.

So my fabulous prize became the biggest dilemma of my life. How do you share two tickets into three people? Do we split the cost of the third ticket between us? No, that's not fair to me, they said. After all, it was my prize I'd won. In the end, my younger daughter told me to give the second ticket to Nicole and go somewhere with her. Michelle didn't want to go anywhere that we were interested in, and after the last holiday together, I think she was more than happy to let us go without her. So with her blessing, we mapped out a plan of where we would go with these business class tickets.

With that mentality of 'these are free so I'll go as far as they can possibly take me', we chose the longest route we could find. The flights had to go via Dubai both ways, that was part of the deal. An English friend suggested "Iceland's lovely that time of year I hear!". We settled on flying into Los Angeles and returning out of New York via Dubai both ways. The long way round, for us in Australia. Big mistake.

I was meant to be meeting up in September with the group from that party night in Spain, it was Lauren's sister's sixtieth birthday and she was celebrating it in Las Vegas. George and I were invited (if we were still friends that is). I timed this holiday to coincide with that. Nicole would meet me in Los Angeles after I'd finished in Vegas with George, and we would make our own way to New York and join another coach tour from there. We were coach tour devotees after that first experience. We'd both always wanted to visit New York and the surrounding states, so this was a perfect plan. We booked the flights and put it all aside. We had a trip to France to get over with first.

It seemed that my daughter and I lived our lives around planning holidays - that was pretty much true. Our jobs were hard work but the rewards when they came were very generous. I am not a materialistic person, so I don't buy 'stuff'. I spend my money on travel and adventure, that's what I love. I'm a Sagittarian, we're born traveller's.

So in between the mundaneness of work, we'd plan our next holiday.

Nicole and I had this romantic notion of buying a run down property in the countryside of France and doing it up for a holiday haven. We spent hours trawling the internet and decided on a region we'd never discovered before. Called the 'Centre' region, just south of Paris, we'd somehow skirted around it on our previous travels. It was beautiful, exactly what we imagined French countryside to look like. And it was cheap - really cheap. Because it wasn't a tourist region, the prices had never risen. We researched everything we could about buying in France, and it was do-able. We even were going to bring Michelle and their father in on it, they were both keen as well. France has a 'law of hereditary' for property, in that if either parent dies, the property automatically goes to the children, regardless of whether there is a new spouse on the scene. Whatever either of us bought, it would always go to the girls. So it made sense to share the cost between the four of us. It was quite an exciting prospect.

With than plan in mind, I decided I would stay in bed and breakfasts for two weeks in this Centre region to explore it and have a look around for a property. After the Anzac day ceremony and a few days in Paris. My plans were open after that, I left the ball in George's court to decide if he wanted to meet up with me somewhere. I planned on being away eight weeks - I can travel on a shoestring, it's not that expensive for me.

Yes, George did want to meet up with me again, he said. So we made more plans. Again I did the choosing, somewhere not too far away from England. I was to be doing enough travelling later that year. He was now working in the UAE again. I chose Ibiza. I'd always heard things about it, I wanted to see for myself.

Again, I arrived in Paris a day before Nicole and her partner. They flew on a different airline and had a stopover in Zurich. So, again I had a night in Paris alone. It always seemed such a shame to me, being in Paris without a lover in the most romantic city of all. No point asking George, I knew what his answer would be. This was my sixth visit to Paris, so I wanted to choose a different area, or arrondissement. Somewhere central. I chose a hotel on the Ile St Louis, right in the centre of the river Seine. Beside the Notre Dame. It was perfect. I couldn't have been more central than that. I had a lovely time on my own, wandering the romantic little streets on the Ile, lining up for a famous Berthillon ice cream and exploring the gorgeous fromageries and patisseries.

When Nicole arrived, I met them at the airport, picked up our hire car and headed straight to the Somme for the Anzac Day ceremony the following morning. It was a very special occasion, there were thousands of Australians all converged on the war cemetery to remember the fallen. And it was freezing! It was a dawn service, France was just coming out of their winter and we shivered through the entire service. Wouldn't have missed it for the world though. The image of the lone bugler playing The Last Post up in the tower with the sun rising behind him will stay in our hearts forever.

The thousands of Australians all converged on the tiny town of Villers-Bretonneux afterwards. It didn't cater for 5000 guests. There was one café and one bakery open in the town, to serve all those hungry mouths. By the time I got served, they had run out of tea bags. A lady behind me in the queue offered me one of hers - she bought her own. We all took turns of sitting and standing. It was chaotic to say the least. But as always, the good natured Aussies just took it all in their stride. We decided there was a huge opportunity screaming out to be filled by an entrepreneurial caterer - set up some marquee's in the park, throw on a barbecue and sausage sizzle, stock up on beer (and tea bags), bring a few Aussie bands on the scene and make a killing. And donate it all back to the little town. Mmm, might think about that, we thought.

We continued on our journey, heading over to the beaches of Normandy. Nicole's partner was interested in all things military and we wanted it to be enjoyable for him, it was his first overseas trip since he was a child. We took a half day tour of the trenches and landing beaches. It was absolutely fascinating, the guide was a young Irish man who lived and breathed World War history. He'd once been part of the IRA. He was also very funny, he had us hanging on his every word. We visited Mont St Michel again - we loved it there. Moules mariniere for lunch - how very French. Stayed in a beautiful 17th century home that we had come across by chance on our last visit to France. The rooms above the old stables were our quarters for a few days - full of antiquities. Below us was a collection of old vintage cars that Mark was fascinated with. Run by a delightful French couple, the house even had a resident ghost, who had introduced himself to us on our previous visit!

Arriving back in Paris, we returned the car and moved to our hotel, the same one in the Latin Quarter we'd stayed in previously with Michelle. We loved the location. Unfortunately we didn't get the same room that had a loft bedroom, so were all just side by side in the one room. Nicole wasn't keen on this set up, not because of a lack of privacy for her and her partner, but because of my snoring! So we had to take separate rooms.

We enjoyed three lovely days in Paris. We did all the usual tourist things, showing it off to Nicole's partner. We both loved Paris. While they visited the Louvre, (I'd seen it three times, I didn't need to go again) I took myself off on a bicycle tour of the city. It was great fun, and a novel way of seeing Paris. I didn't stack it once, I was proud of myself. I treated us all to a night river cruise. So romantic for them, but not for me, on my own.

I joined them for the transfer to the airport, where they flew out for their luxury tour of Canada and I picked up my hire car. It was the tiniest little Peugeot I'd ever seen, we don't have them back in Australia. I was surprised it fitted my suitcase in, it was so small. But I ended up loving it, this cute little black zippy thing that kept up with the best of them on the motorways. I headed off to the Centre region, where I'd booked a bed and breakfast for a week.

I drove through a thunderstorm on the motorway, and couldn't work out how to get the wipers to stay on. So I trundled along at 100 kph with the wipers on intermittent! Eventually I found out how they worked but not before I nearly killed myself on the road.

I found my b and b, it was gorgeous. A converted barn, just like what we had in mind to buy, I was going to love my week here. I explored every little town and village in the region, it was delightful. Made myself known to a few estate agents and had a look at a couple of properties. But then reality set in. After I got over the beauty of the region and the quaintness of a run down stone barn to consider renovating, it occurred to me that there was *nothing* to do in these little villages. Even less in the hamlets of five or six houses.

After four nights at home in the b and b with nowhere to go - the village had one restaurant, a post box and a public telephone - I realized I would die of boredom in a country holiday cottage. The days dragged, there's only so many hours you can spend driving around the countryside. I would arrive back mid afternoon and wonder what to do with myself. The owners little dog Molly, never had so many walks before I arrived. I'd never done so much reading. What did these people do for entertainment, I wondered? I was climbing the walls by the time my week was up. I emailed Nicole. "I can't do it, we'll have to shelve the idea of buying in the country. We would kill each other with boredom" I wrote her.

I was meant to have another week in another bed and breakfast in a different section of the Centre region. I cancelled the booking and took myself off to the south of France to a fantastic, 'bustling' city called Montpellier, in the Languedoc region. I found a studio flat on the internet for a fraction of what it was going to cost me to stay in the b and b. George wasn't flying into London for another week, other-wise we would have met up earlier.

What a great place. A university city, so it had people bustling about everywhere. This was more like it. I ditched the hire car, I didn't need it here. Plenty to do of a night, even just watching buskers in the 'Place de la Comedie', the main square in town. There were two tram lines, with brightly coloured trams. One line had blue swallows, the other bright flowers painted all over the carriages so you could tell which line you were on. The tram stopped right outside my door. I was alongside a beautiful canal that ran through the city, with stunning modern buildings either side of it. I visited beaches and markets, picking up a gorgeous bikini for five euros. I visited a bullring showing 'la course des Taureaux', a bull-run event where fit young men chase a bull around the ring attempting to grab a ribbon from its horns. Not like the barbaric bullfight, just a bit tormenting for the bull. And painful for the guys who didn't get out of its way quick enough.

I counted down the days, George and I couldn't wait to see each other again.

Chapter 21

Hole in the Wall

No stretch limousine greeting me at the airport this time. Just a happy George. He'd organised a hire car and we headed down to Brighton. I had booked us into a darling bed and breakfast and had organised with the owners to have a bottle of champagne on ice ready on arrival. To my amusement, she'd ordered an Australian bottle of Jacob's Creek for me. The usual pattern followed - polish off the champagne, a couple of hours of lovemaking and out to explore the town. We loved having sex together, we always bought out the 'best' in each other. And it was always fun. I don't just mean fun sex, but belly aching fun from George's jokes and witty one liners.

We hit the town again, Brighton is a great place for a night out. We visited the comedy club (of course) then found ourselves in some gay bars. The first was a lesbian bar, and again I was hit on - I wish I attracted men the same way I seemed to attract women. They loved us though when they realised I was definitely straight - we had an hilarious time with them. Then somehow got coaxed into a gay cabaret bar by a gorgeous, funny transvestite who gave us tickets to her show. She had legs to die for! Then another bar where it was George's turn to be hit on. In all this hilarity we had forgotten about dinner.

We ended up pinching some hot chips from a group of young girls on our way back to our room. They felt sorry for us.

Fortunately, we left these premises in the same state we found them, the owners would be pleased to know. On a previous overnight stay in Brighton, (before flying to Cyprus) we stayed in a very old hotel on the seafront. Once again, we arrived back a bit intoxicated - we weren't alcoholics, its just that our nights out always went on till the wee hours of the morning, so we would consume quite a lot of alcohol. George flopped onto the bed in a drunken stupor. In my efforts to get him under the quilt, I rolled him off the bed and his shoulder went straight through the plaster wall. We fell about in hysterics. I cleaned the mess as best I could and we high tailed it out of there the next morning before the cleaners arrived to discover the hole in the wall. We can never return to that hotel again, fair to say.

A further couple of nights were spent in another seaside town I had earmarked as a good place for me to buy my 'bolt hole' for my future retirement. I explored both the old and new town , inspected a couple of properties and decided it was definitely the right place for me. It ticked all the boxes - on the seafront (Aussies are 'coast dwellers', we can't be too far from the beach), it was close to London and had easy access to Gatwick airport for my future jaunts over to the continent. And it was affordable - most importantly. I would work on making it happen when I returned home.

George had planned a driving tour of England, to places I hadn't been before. We spent the next week travelling the length and breadth of the country. It was like his nostalgia tour, showing me the places he went to as a child. No planned route, we just found a place to stay when we got there. Whitby in the north, where he'd spent his childhood summers. The obligatory photo of me in front of the Captain Cook statue- my girls would love this, it was a standing joke about me always having my photos taken in front of a statue. Over to his home town, stopping on the way at the scene of the 'Heartbeat' series for a drink in the 'Aidensfield Arms', and a visit to his home town cemetery. He hadn't visited his parent's grave's for years, I felt very privileged to be part of this poignant moment for him.

He took me to my first football match. I loved it. It was his team on their home ground. I had always wanted to see an English football game. I wasn't disappointed. The atmosphere was electric, football is a religion to die-hard fans. Over to the Lakes district. We visited the Laurel and Hardy museum, another photo beside the statue of them. George had been carrying around an autograph of Stan Laurel - it was actually a signed utility bill cheque - and wanted the museum to have it. They agreed on a price and made the exchange. A television crew happened to be filming there, this new museum had just opened and they interviewed George about his autograph. "Another bloody audience!" I thought to myself. Can we never go anywhere without attracting one?

Down to Liverpool again. I toured the Beatles museum at the docks while George enjoyed a coffee and read the paper. I bought a Beatles postcard and joined him for a coffee. As I was writing on the card to send it to my friend Lauren who was from Liverpool, a *very* famous and valuable (and really cute Spaniard) Liverpool footballer sat down beside me, we almost touched shoulders. George had already pointed him out to me. He couldn't help himself. He excused himself to this revered player and explained that I was writing to my friend in Australia who was a massive Liverpool supporter, from Liverpool. Could I have his autograph on the postcard? Of course I could, he was very gracious. It was a wonderful moment. I had to add a PS to Lauren on the postcard, to explain that this really was his autograph. Don't throw this card away, I warned her! She and her son were thrilled to pieces.

Back to London. Always more fun with George, I couldn't resist a few nights in my new favourite city. We found a great little studio apartment in Bayswater just around the corner from Hyde Park. We spent a lovely day wandering through this beautiful park. George took me to see his favourite play 'Blood Brothers'. He still cried at the end, even though he'd seen it five times before. We met an actor in a pub, I knew him from 'The Vicar of Dibley', he was better known as 'Trigger' in 'Only Fools and Horses' - he graciously swapped his autograph for a spare stool. We spotted a few more famous British actresses, it was post-theatre drinks time for them. One night we stopped by a nearby pub for dinner.

We passed a group of people sitting outside as I walked up to view the menu board and proceeded to head inside. George caught up to me. "You've no idea who you just passed outside, do you?" No, I didn't.

"Robbie Williams" he said.

By the time I flew out the door, he had walked off with his mates.

We attended another football match when we returned to London, this time an 'away' game for his team. It was more incredible than that first game to watch. The fans, not the game. His team lost, they always did. The costumes that some of the fans wore were outrageous, and I didn't realise that the 'away' fans were allowed to stand up for the duration of the game. The football chants swung back and forth between the two sets of fans, it was an amazing spectacle to watch. It was a real treat for me, this kind of singing at matches back home just doesn't occur.

We had met up with some of his old football fan mates at a pub before the match. George was in fine form, telling his jokes and acting it up, he hadn't seen these fellows for quite a while.

"How do you put up with him?" one of them asked me.

"In very small doses" I replied.

Chapter 22

Passion Killer

The following day we flew to Ibiza. We travelled really well together, both very used to flying so we took all the mayhem that happens prior to boarding in our stride. Always very relaxed and usually the last to board, we were very casual about it.

We had booked a hotel in the San Antonio Bay area of the island. My English friends back home were horrified when I told them where I was going.

"That's a wild party town, you'll hate it there", they warned. They obviously didn't know the other side of me.

Our hotel room was lovely with an amazing view of the beach below and right across the bay. It was stunning. Problem was, it had two single beds. I presented myself to reception.

"Excuse me, but there's been some mistake. I requested a queen bed, can you find us another room please?"

"Sorry senora, we have very few rooms with queen beds, they're nearly all twin beds" they informed me. An odd situation I thought.

"We'll see if we can locate a room suitable for you" they continued.

They did call back in a short while. "The only room available with a queen bed is on the opposite side of the hall and has a view of the road only" they informed us.

We weren't prepared to give up our beautiful view.

"Thank you, we'll make do with what we've got." I replied.

No problems, we'll just push the beds together. No big deal really.

It wasn't long before we were on the beach. Out through a gate in the pool area, and straight onto the sand. It was idyllic. And dangerous. For right beside this gateway, was a fabulous beach bar with a super friendly owner named Luis. Who made the most incredible jugs of sangria with about five different types of alcohol mixed in.

We were in for some fun times, we guessed already.

That first afternoon, we consumed two jugs of this magic elixir. We became as horny as hell. I don't know what Luis put in this mix, but it had a wonderful effect on us. We headed up to our room. We pushed the beds together. With me on one side and George on the other side of the join, we engaged in some serious foreplay. With a magnificent erection at the ready, George made his move to mount me. The beds parted. Down he went, flat on his face. And his erect penis.

Well, I've never laughed so much in my life. We were both hysterical. This time I think I did wet myself. The jokes started:

"I knew we were drifting apart, but this is ridiculous";

"When I said I wanted a separation, this wasn't what I had in mind"

On and on they came, both of us outwitting the other. Half an hour later I was still convulsing with laughter. Every time I tried to contain myself, it started over again. George took photos of me, he'd never seen me laugh so much.

Suffice to say, we couldn't continue with the sex.

We ventured into town that night after dinner. We had made our booking as a 'half board' package, so breakfast and dinners were included. I had read on the internet about the beautiful sunsets on the island. They didn't disappoint. We watched from a rocky ledge along the beach as the sun lowered itself for another day. A long thin purple cloud passed in front, breaking open a slit just enough so this vast orange ball appeared above, in the middle and below the cloud. It was a magnificent sight. Definitely a Kodak moment. We continued our stroll into town.

It was definitely a party town! But I'd hardly call it 'wild' as my friends had warned me. I always find it a shame that people make foregone conclusions about a place, based on what usually is an urban myth. Without ever having been to the area themselves. San Antonio was a great place. Lively and colourful, full of people of all ages just out having a good time. There were lots of stag do's and hen's groups but they were just enjoying themselves. As young people should.

The following nights were spent venturing into and out of numerous bars playing all manner of music. Playing darts in an English pub with the landlord. Karaoke bars - I still couldn't do it. George sang 'Maggie May' again. And an old favourite of his, 'You Make Me Feel Brand New', by the Stylistics. I didn't know he could sing falsetto. Why was I surprised? Again, we met lots of people and made some lovely friends.

One night, we returned to a particularly atmospheric bar with a guy playing bongo drums and another playing saxophone. The music was mesmerizing. I kicked my shoes off, and we both just moved to the music, I wouldn't call it dancing. Our bodies just took over, to the beat of the drums. It was intoxicating, I'd never experienced a feeling like it.

We had befriended a couple at our beach bar that we became great friends with. We would meet up with them every afternoon for the magic sangria. The boys moved onto beers eventually. They were great fun. She would proudly tell us that before she divorced her previous (wealthy) husband, she made sure she got her teeth and a boob job done. She was so proud of her beautiful breasts, all part of her divorce settlement.

They were very friendly with some of the beach vendors, falling victim to their persuasive ways and had purchased numerous watches and sunglasses from these African men. George ended up weakening and also bought a fake Rolex, just to keep them happy. We would meet them after dinner in town, at their local bar near their hotel. One night George got so drunk he disappeared to the toilet and fell asleep on it. I had to walk him into town for some food, all he wanted was chips in curry sauce.

Our new found friends, after hearing our hilarious story of our sex mishap, asked how we overcame the separating beds syndrome. We turned the mattresses around so they lay sideways across the beds. I must send that solution into 'Martha's Helpful Hints'.

The two of us hired a car for the day to explore a bit more of the region. Ibiza is a beautiful island, quite mountainous in places. We discovered a little hidden bay on the northern side of the island. Quite a few steps led down to this beach, it was very picturesque with aqua blue waters. We enjoyed a beautiful lunch in a beachside restaurant, then hired a sunbed for a sunbake and a bit of a siesta. It wasn't long before the warmth of the sun lured us into the sea to cool off. The waters were pristine. We swam and frolicked like children again, we both loved the sea.

All of a sudden, I felt a fierce pain as something brushed past me. I shrieked. I splashed and floundered around in the water. Poor George wondered what was happening. I had been stung by a jellyfish. As we hurriedly made our way into shore, we noticed dozens of them around us, they must have all just washed in on a wave. By the time I reached the sand, I had a welt on the inside of my arm in the shape of its body and two of its tentacles. About six inches long. And it started stinging. Badly.

We approached the owner of the bar on the beach and he provided me with a bottle of vinegar and a wad of paper towels to soak it in. By this time another young woman had come up, she had been stung too. I held the soaking towels over the sting for about half an hour. The whole area had blistered by this time and I was in a lot of pain. Neither of us knew anything about these types of jellyfish - were they poisonous? Were they deadly even? The barman didn't think so, it happens often he told us. That was comforting. So once again, George had to keep an eye on me for the rest of the day to see if I had any reaction to the sting.

He was becoming paranoid. Every time we went on holiday it seemed, something would happen to me. Again, we imagined what kind of explanation he would give my girls if this turned serious. I was becoming a liability!

The pain from that sting lasted for three days before it subsided. I rode it out with painkillers and alcohol. The welt could still be seen six months later. Nasty little critters.

Our week passed too quickly, we were at the beach bar next to our hotel for a last afternoon with our friends. Donna and I were now onto our fourth jug of sangria. It was too easy to drink. George disappeared up to our room to get a wrap for me, it was getting cool.

When he returned, he had somehow borrowed an arm full of watches and sunglasses from one of the sellers who'd got to know us. He'd donned his Jamaican beanie with the dreadlocks and came back to us pretending to be one of the beach vendors. "Wanna buy a watch mon?" he joked with us, showing a row of watches the length of his arm. "Very good price for you today!"

He then produced a red Fez hat out of a bag, complete with tufts of black hair sprouting from it. He proceeded to entertain the three of us with a full Tommy Cooper routine, complete with props. As you can imagine, it wasn't long before we had another three couples pull up their chairs to watch this spectacle. We had a great laugh. Even people further away who couldn't hear him were laughing at his antics. Luis the bar owner treated us to another round of drinks. It was the funniest thing that had ever happened at his bar. George gave him his Jamaican beanie with the dreadlocks.

We'd made more friends. Somehow, I ended up with photos on my camera of us posing with these new friends, and I have no memory of them being taken. We were pretty intoxicated by the end of this afternoon. After more rounds of drinks from his audience! We concluded that we had consumed eight jugs of sangria in that session!

We made arrangements to meet up with everyone later, in town. We went in for our dinner. Apparently I ate a full dinner, according to George. I had no recollection of that either. On returning to our hotel room, he suggested I have a bit of a nap before we head out again. I woke up at 11 o'clock that night. We both had slept through our meeting up with our friends. We never saw them again, it was our last night.

The next morning before we packed, George showed me a video he had taped while I slept the night before. He'd managed to get me half undressed, but couldn't remove my top - I was out cold.

This video showed me half naked and snoring so loudly I could have woken the dead. He was tickling me with a feather and not just under my nose! He thought it was hilarious. He would. I made sure he deleted it - I knew his sense of humour too well.

Chapter 23

It's a Small World After All

Next stop, Barcelona. Four days and nights in a hotel on the famous Las Ramblas, the main thoroughfare in the city. We loved it there, the tree lined street has a promenade running through the centre with restaurants, flower sellers and street performers along the length of it. Always something to watch. We discovered the Sant Josep market, an amazing colourful spectacle of fresh fruit and vegetables and a fish market. We visited the market every day for a serving of fresh fruit salad, our contribution to healthy eating. We would hand one of these fruit salads to the old beggar woman out the front.

We popped into an Australian bar one night. I chatted to the delightful blonde girl behind the bar - she was an Aussie. What a small world we live in. Somehow we ended up talking about the beaches south of Sydney and I explained that I had spent my childhood years holidaying in a 'shack' owned by my family, on the beach at Coalcliff. Whole generations of families used these weekenders for over 40 years. My own parents met there before the war, their parents had been the founders of this little holiday community.

"My grandparents owned a shack at Coalcliff as well, my mum spent her childhood there just like you! " Lucy informed me.

"What were their names? I knew a lot of families at Coalcliff" I asked her excitedly.

"Lucy and Jim Pickering. My mum's name is Therese. Have you heard of them?"

I stood there dumbfounded. I started laughing.

"They were our next door neighbours! Our doors were twelve feet apart. Therese was my best friend! We were both the youngest in the families." I exclaimed to her.

Unbelievable! Here I was on the other side of the world in a pub, and run into the daughter of a childhood friend. George was as excited as I was - he'd heard my story about Coalcliff many times, I had wonderful childhood memories of my days there.

Of coarse, photos were taken and email addresses were swapped. I was so excited.

Barcelona has a beautiful beach. We couldn't resist our love of the sea and spent a couple of afternoons sunbathing and swimming in the warm waters. Unfortunately, Barcelona's beaches are spoilt by a never ending parade of beach vendors, selling anything from coconut juice to dresses. All walking incessantly between sunbathers, calling out their presence. It drove me insane. It really was an invasion of privacy. Beaches are meant to be a relaxing haven to spend some quiet time, not be bombarded by noisy annoying hawkers. Some of the young girls were offering massages and this was obviously an illegal practice. The police arrived and these women suddenly turned into sunbathers, sometimes hiding amongst a group of genuine beach goers so as not to be noticed. It made me appreciate my beautiful beach culture back home.

On to Benidorm for a week. This was the first time we had actually stayed in the town. Our other visits had only been for a night out, we had stayed in Calpe. We both love Benidorm. Another of those places whose reputation precedes it, most people describing the place as tacky and full of obscene Brits on a drinking binge. I beg to differ. Beautiful beaches and countryside, a quaint old town and a nightlife with something for everyone. I always say to people who look at me in horror when I tell them where I am going - "where else in the world can you find non stop entertainment for free, all for just the cost of a drink?" Nowhere I've ever been before.

Chapter 24

Home Alone

Our holiday came to an end. This time was different though. Or meant to be. George's three year ban was up. We had planned for him to return to Australia with me and stay the allowable three months while we set about settling in together and applying for a permanent visa for him. We were finally going to be able to be together. It was what we had both realised we wanted. We would stopover in Bangkok for a few days on the way home. With this plan in place, George had applied for a tourist visa some weeks before. His airfare had been booked and paid for, he would arrive on a different flight an hour later than me. Back on Australian soil at last.

His application was turned down - he'd applied too soon. They suggested he apply in person in London for a different visitor visa. We followed all the procedures. However, this one was going to take three to five weeks to process. I couldn't stay on any longer, I needed to get home to work. We cancelled the Bangkok stopover and changed his flight dates.

Again, we had to say our goodbyes at the airport, where I flew home utterly dejected. He had no home to go to, his job in the UAE had come to an abrupt halt when the site shut down with no warning. He had given up his apartment as he hadn't intended returning, he was coming to Australia with me. It was heart wrenching for him. With nowhere to go, he boarded with a mate and managed to find some work to keep him going until he could finally fly out to me.

Things were different for me at home this time. We had declared our love for each other and our wish to marry, once and for all. I went about my days with happy anticipation of what our lives would be like when George arrived. My friends were eager to meet him finally, and were thrilled for me. It was obvious that even though things hadn't worked out in the past, we clearly loved each other - we kept going back to each other. Were we soul mates? Life partners? We thought so. This 'thing' we had wasn't going away. We couldn't wait to finally set up house, in Australia.

George's visa was turned down again. They were not going to let him back in the country on a temporary visa, he would have to wait till he qualified for a permanent visa. We were devastated, again.

We were going to have to wait until he could apply for a fiance visa, with an 'intention to marry' me. This was the quickest type of visa available to him. And we did want to marry. He wanted me to be his real wife, not a pretend one. He couldn't apply for this type of visa however, until he had divorced Jane. The whole procedure was now going to take around nine months, we calculated. It was so disappointing.

So once again, we had to make new plans. This time we did call each other a couple of times a week, we were both gutted. He wrote to the visa application department, pleading his case. I sent a very well worded email to the woman who had turned down his application, expressing my dismay at her decision when too many 'undesirables' were granted permanent visas into my country. I sent the email to George first, for his approval. I didn't want to antagonize the situation.

"You should be Gordon Brown's speech writer. That is brilliant - send it to her" he replied. Good thing I wasn't Gordon Brown's speech writer - I'd be out of a job now!

We decided that we couldn't be apart for nine months. I would come over to England for Christmas. Finally, a Christmas together. And I had always wanted a white Christmas - or a cold one at least, even without the snow. He managed to secure a good job and would move into his own flat prior to me arriving. In the meantime, he set about applying for his divorce. Jane had finally agreed to it, much to our relief. It made it easier under UK law. We set a date for our marriage for one year from now. Where would we get married, we wondered? George's suggestion of Las Vegas wasn't received with quite the reaction he had hoped for. No tacky chapel wedding for me, I told him. We had plenty of time to decide, it was the least of our worries.

I kept an eye on airfares, I knew that flying to the UK a few days before Christmas was going to be an expensive exercise, so kept a lookout for specials. I found one, incredibly cheap, with a stopover in Japan included in the price. I booked it and paid a deposit. I would stay till the end of January, that would leave about another four months before George could come to Australia.

It was during this time that Nicole and I decided that we could not realistically afford to take more time off for the trip we had planned with the free tickets. She was saving for a trip with her partner, I was saving for my life with George. I was able to change the dates and passenger details of my prize tickets. I pushed the date back as late as I could and nominated George as the other passenger. We would still go to Las Vegas and New York, and if he wasn't in Australia by then he would join the flight in Dubai. The new dates and names were locked in. I would not be able to change them again, I was told. No problems, I assured them. No need for any more changes.

With four months to go till Christmas, I was offered to house-sit and care-take a large waterfront home that was now empty as the tenant's had vacated. This home belonged to some very dear friends of mine, I had sold it to them some three years before, then sold them into another home that was more suitable to their needs. Both well into their eighties now, he had been a famous entertainer in his day. They were a delightful couple and we became very close friends. He and I had a great rapport, he loved my sense of humour and would serenade to me whenever I drove him to doctor's appointments or such things. His wife was adorable, we were like best friends. She jokingly told me once that they were so fond of me, she was going to leave him to me in her will. Oh joy, I told her. A fifty something year old man who loved being the life of the party I could handle, but an eighty five year old? I wasn't so sure. They were great fun to be around. Still walked arm in arm - how romantic. "We're propping each other up" she would say to me.

She arranged that I would move into the house while it was on the market to be sold, and if that didn't happen just prior to me leaving for Christmas with George, we would put tenants back in it. The timing worked well for me, so I moved my furniture and belongings into their enormous house and floated around in a mansion for a while, alone. George would have loved it if he'd been able to come over. It had a snooker table and home theatre, a beautiful pool and a jetty. I felt very privileged to be looking after it for them.

I gave up the apartment I was living in, as I was to move into my investment house (George's old house) when I returned after Christmas, in preparation for George's arrival. The plan was to renovate the house to make it more comfortable.

Weeks passed by, both of us busy with work. Each time we spoke, I checked that it was still fine for me to come at Christmas and that he would have somewhere for me to stay.

"I need to pay my airfare by the end of September, so if you don't think it's a good idea for me to come, you need to tell me" I told him one night.

Of course he still wanted me to come, he said. He was looking forward to our first Christmas together. Not as much as I am, I thought to myself.

Within six weeks of me moving into the mansion, the family of the owners decided they didn't like the agreement their mother had made with me, and asked me to leave so they could put tenant's back in and regain some income. I was out on the street, quite literally. I had nowhere to go, my own tenant couldn't be removed from my house. With only eight weeks till I went away for Christmas, I couldn't sign another lease. Fortunately, I had a great circle of friends, and one of them offered for me to stay with her for as long as necessary. So I was on the move again. With my furniture back in storage, I was beginning to feel like a gypsy. All part of life's great adventure, I told myself.

I settled in to my friend's house, this was not something I was used to. I had lived on my own for the last five years. It worked out well though, we were both hardly ever home. We had very busy social lives and sometimes wouldn't see each other for days. We would leave notes for each other on the hall table with updates.

A girlfriend and I booked a day trip on a tall ship one day. We left the pier at around eight thirty in the morning and set sail for Stradbroke Island, a popular surfing and picnicking island. We decided it would be a nice treat to have a bottle of champagne during the trip, it seemed so appropriate on this beautiful old sailing ship. Most of our fellow guests were quite a bit older than us or overseas tourists, so we spent the entire journey explaining that we 'don't usually drink alcohol this early in the day.' Whether they believed us or not, I don't know. We certainly looked like old hands at this kind of thing. The picnic spot was beautiful, we swam and sunbathed when we arrived. Enjoyed a great barbecue lunch and entertainment. And more champagne.

A fellow came along touting for passengers for his sea-plane flights. We decided we would go, it sounded like fun. We were teamed up with one other couple - the plane only held five people in total. She was terrified of flying, so was sat beside the pilot to become his co-pilot and actually took the controls for a bit. Her husband had a broken leg which was in plaster and he hobbled aboard on crutches.

The plane set off out onto the wide part of the Broadwater, it needed a decent length of water for takeoff. Then came to a sudden stop. The pilot had run into a sand bar! He was bogged! He alighted and tried to push the plane off the sand, but it didn't budge. So, us three women had to hoist up our skirts and push our plane out of the sandbar. While hubby with the broken leg could only sit and watch. And laugh. The guys on shore finally arrived on jet skis to help, but we had already freed it by then.

We had a great laugh. The pilot was very apologetic and gave us an extra long flight.

I have a very long 'bucket list' of things to do before I die, but pushing a seaplane out of a sandbar hadn't been one of them. Until now. It could only happen to me!

Chapter 25

"He's Just Not That Into You"

A few phone calls to George went unanswered for a couple of weeks. When we did speak, he was a little elusive and asked me to call back the next night for a chat. He didn't answer when I called back. I tried from a different phone number. He answered, then pretended he couldn't hear me and hung up. I could hear him fine and there was a lot of noise in the background. Clearly he didn't want to have this chat he mentioned. I didn't hear from him after that night.

He'd done it to me again. Disappeared on me. Heartbreak number five. Or six? My reaction to this swung between sheer rage and heartbreak. I was so sick of the way he just 'turned off the tap' on me, with no reason. I of course emailed him a couple of times just briefly, telling him that I deserved some sort of explanation.

This time I *was* humiliated. Totally humiliated. I couldn't tell my friends. Only my daughters knew, I had to tell them. But everyone in my life knew of my love for this man and knew how excited I was that finally we would be together. Even the girls in my local bank, clients, colleagues - all had been following this romance since it started. How could I tell them he's done it to me again. It was more than I could bear.

I even went away on an all girl cruise with seven friends without telling any of them, I couldn't face the pity they would bestow on me, and trying to match make me with some other man. I didn't want to be mollycoddled. Or lectured to.

After a month, he did email me with his interpretation of an excuse. He had heard from the immigration department and had been told he was now banned from entering Australia for another ten years as punishment for overstaying his visa. So had to abandon his dream of living in Oz. Threw in the towel. Decided it was time to move on. Without me. Oh, and 'have a great Christmas' he finished off with!

I was dumbstruck. How do I respond to that? I emailed him of course, this time with three different reactions, all in the one email. Firstly, I asked how he could possibly think I'd have a 'great Christmas' after what he had just done to me. Secondly, a written tirade of where I fitted into his dream of living in Australia, or didn't I? And was this 'banned for ten years' just an excuse to cover up the real reason why he'd given up on me? My third reaction came from my heart. I asked him if this was what he really wanted - to end our relationship - because obstacles were put in his way. What if we were really the love of each other's lives, I asked him. What if we truly were soul mates, and one of us threw in the towel because it just got too hard to be together? And worse still, that the other just let it happen without a fight. So, I told him I would still be coming to England for Christmas, and this would be his chance to make up if he didn't want *us* to end.

True to form, I didn't get a reply. After much agonising, I had decided to still go to England for Christmas. I had already paid for my flight just a week before George did his latest disappearing act. And 'being dumped' didn't fit into the criteria for lodging a claim on my travel insurance. Besides, I had been wanting to experience a white Christmas - or at least a cold one - for so long. I couldn't let this man and his despicable actions ruin that part of my plans. He'd just ruined every other plan I had made for my life.

This time my daughters didn't hold their tongue. Who could blame them really? They had watched this man break my heart too many times over the last four and a half years, they were having no more of it. And they agreed I should still go, I would be miserable and angry if I didn't and just spoil everyone else's Christmas.

So new plans were made. I had a number of friends in England that I could visit. My youngest daughter had friends in Northern Ireland. When they heard of my plight, they invited me to stay with them for a week, they would show me around county Antrim. My friend Lauren's sister was visiting her daughter in Liverpool, so I booked to stay nearby and they would show me more of the city. I loved Liverpool, so was happy to visit again. I would call on the couple we met in Ibiza, they were thrilled to hear from me. Not so thrilled to hear what

George had done. And friends I had met in Australia were starring in a pantomime of Cinderella, they arranged for a ticket for me. I had never seen a panto before, so was excited about seeing them on stage.

Gradually my friends at home found out, one by one. I would only tell them if they asked about George and how our plans were going. They were all shocked and so sorry for me. They knew how much he meant to me, how all my future plans revolved around being with him. They also knew how humiliating it was for me to tell them.

My seaplane buddy invited me to her apartment by the beach for some time out. She knew how therapeutic my walks along the beach were to me. I was pampered all weekend, she was wonderful. Pedicures, massages, facials, lovely girly things. She casually left a copy of the book 'He's Just Not That Into You' on the coffee table, hoping it would catch my eye. It did. I opened up to the chapter 'He's just not that into you if he…….. disappears on you.' We had a good laugh.

Chapter 26

What's It All About, Alfie?

Departure day neared. I had had plenty of time to rethink my plans for my future. I needed to set new goals, the last goalposts were not just moved on me, but completely *re*moved. Along with the strain and disappointment of George's actions, my business was also becoming a struggle. I decided I would close it down for good on my birthday. It had become too stressful, I was a little fish in a big sea of competition. I would go and work for one of my rivals when I returned from England.

So I looked on my approaching fifty fifth birthday as the start of a new life, or chapter in my life. I can't pretend I wasn't still hurting about George - never a day went by that I didn't yearn to have him back. But I knew I wouldn't, or couldn't. I couldn't put myself through the heartache again. Still battered and bruised, but so angry with him at the same time. How dare he just throw me away like a dirty dish-rag. Not for the first time. But definitely the last, I told myself.

On the night of my birthday just days before my departure, I had been out for drinks with the girls. When I arrived home, I decided to check on one of those social networking sites to see what George had been up to. To my surprise, I found he had updated his 'status' about himself. 'Living in Cyprus, married to the lovely Jane, etc, etc'. I sat and stared at it. Is this some sort of joke? Had his daughter put it on there for some reason? I didn't know what to think. I'll leave it, I decided, in case it's some sort of mistake. I'll wait to see if I hear from him. Great birthday present!

I arrived in London a few days before Christmas. In that last email to George I had given him details of where I was staying and what dates, if he did want to 'make-up', or discuss things. He didn't turn up of course. Probably a good thing, my heart was mending, seeing him would have just undone all the healing that had occurred.

But I was livid. And gutted. What sort of double life had this man been living? Was he back with Jane, or had he never actually left her? All sorts of scenarios played around in my mind. Had I just been taken for a ride all this time, or had he gone back to her after the upsetting news about his visa being rejected? I sent an email and I didn't hold back. It was the most scathing email I had ever sent to anyone, I was so angry and utterly humiliated. At the end of the email, I asked him one favour.

"Could you remove the 'married to the lovely Jane' from your profile page just long enough for my daughters to forget your name. To spare them the humiliation of knowing what a fool their mother has been" I ended with. He did remove it, but I didn't hear from him. Not surprised.

I wasn't completely alone on this trip though. My 'seaplane' friend's partner had a very tired and worn looking (stuffed) monkey from his childhood, that had only recently been re-discovered after having spent the last twenty years locked in a box. 'Alfie' had accompanied us on our Melbourne Cup all girl cruise, attending formal dinners on board, a road trip to Torquay and various other activities much to the amusement of our other cabin friends. Alfie was a bit light on clothes, so for formal night we 'borrowed' a pair of black knickers from one of the girls, made a bow tie to complement his white shirt that he had, fashioned some black boots out of a shopping bag and sat him at the dinner table with us. He became a bit of a celebrity.

So I began teasing Lisa's partner about taking Alfie to England with me for Christmas. "He's been locked away in a box for twenty years, it's time he got out to see the world", I joked to him. The joke carried on for a few weeks, until it was time for me to go. "Come on now, he's the only male I can trust at the moment, you've got to let him come with me" I pleaded jokingly with his owner. And so Alfie became my travel partner - he was off to see the world! He had his own little case of clothes and we made up a little passport for him. Unfortunately, he had to endure the flight stashed in my suitcase, so he missed the stopover in Japan. I made up for it though, I bought him his own little kimono.

If I thought London was fantastic on my previous visits, then this time was just magical. It had snowed a couple of days before I arrived, and snow was still on the ground in Hyde Park. My hotel was again just across the road from there, I liked that particular part of London. It was close to the Tube and buses, and it was safe. So Alfie and I experienced our first snow in England. I took Alfie with me wherever I could.

First stop though was Oxford Street to buy a winter coat. I didn't own anything warm enough for English winters. I knew what I wanted - a white puff jacket, knee length to keep me warm all over. I found the exact thing in Primark, for a fraction of what I had expected to pay. I went a bit crazy with shopping in there, it became my new favourite store. Then realized I would have to post everything back home, my suitcase was already up to its weight limit. So what I saved on purchases I spent on postage.

I'd booked a number of activities before I left. I watched a Christmas play at Shakespeare's Globe Theatre, seated up in the old balconies. I saw a Carols by Candlelight concert at the Royal Albert Hall, the orchestra dressed in period costume. It was magnificent. Attended the musical 'Jersey Boys' on my second night, I was a bit jetlagged though and kept nodding off during the show. Took Alfie to the Winter Wonderland in Hyde Park and rode the ferris wheel. Rode the double decker buses through Oxford and Regent streets at night to see the Christmas lights. Amazing!

My Christmas day was just brilliant. I called my girls and my sisters early morning. I had some presents to open, I had bought them with me so I wouldn't feel left out. I then set off on foot (no public transport in London on Christmas day) with Alfie and walked to Westminster Pier. We stopped along the way at the Australian War Memorial and Buckingham Palace. Just as I approached the Mall in front of the palace, the changing of the guard was just finishing, so the timing was wonderful. I hadn't expected to see that on the day. When I approached the pier, the bells from Westminster Abbey peeled. It was midday, they rang out for about fifteen minutes. I felt truly blessed that my timing was so perfect to have heard such a beautiful sound.

I had booked a lunchtime cruise for my first Christmas away from home. What better way to celebrate the day than cruising the Thames on a beautiful boat taking in the sights of London? It was perfect - a roast turkey meal, entertainment on board and lovely people for company. Alfie was introduced to the family I was seated with, photos were taken and we had a wonderful day. At the end of the cruise, I managed to catch the last half hour of a boy's choir singing in Westminster Abbey at the end of a service. A final few photos of me and Alfie in front of the palace - he attracted a lot of attention, another bloody male who steals the limelight I thought to myself! The walk home took about an hour, it was dark toward the end and I didn't fancy walking through Hyde Park alone, so took the long way round. I flopped into bed and didn't wake till the next morning.

The week between Christmas and New Year was spent travelling by train to Torquay in Devon and exploring the region. I visited a gorgeous village of thatched cottages and a wonderful pub that my friend Lauren had once worked at. I took Alfie to a miniature village in a nearby town that had been set up all in snow, it was beautiful. Had a real 'Devonshire' tea with ginger scones and clotted cream one day. Divine.

I then travelled up to a town in the midlands to see my friends and watch their Pantomime. Not really knowing what to expect from a panto, I absolutely loved it. It was so professional, the set and the costumes were fabulous. My friends stole the show. They have been working as a comedy double for over thirty years and are well known in the UK. Their humour was very much 'double entendre' so went over the children's heads, but delighted the adult audience. I joined the cast after the show for drinks, one was a famous actor from the Neighbours series. Alfie of course stole the limelight again, appearing in everyone's photos. Headed back into London again.

New Year's Eve was spent on Waterloo Bridge to view the fireworks. I knew I would have to arrive early to secure a good position. I couldn't get in anywhere to eat on the way there, so ended up buying a salad from the local Tesco supermarket and a couple of drinks. What I hadn't calculated though was how long three hours can drag out to when you have to stand in the one place. I couldn't leave my spot, I had a fantastic vantage point on the bridge and didn't want to lose it. I had to stop drinking my drinks, I wouldn't be able to go to a toilet if I kept drinking. It was worth the wait, the fireworks were magnificent. They were set off on the London Eye, it was quite a spectacle. Just as the fireworks finished, it started snowing. How magical! My first snowfall. At New Year. My guardian angels were really spoiling me this trip. Making up for the sadness of being alone, I thought. I thanked them.

The journey home that night was hectic to say the least. Thousands of people all cramming into the entrance to the nearest Tube station. All well behaved though, but very claustrophobic. I was glad I hadn't bought Alfie along, it would have been a bit much for him I thought. He would have gone ape.

New Year's day in London, I travelled up to Hampstead Heath and wandered through the huge park. Then onto Regent's Park and a glimpse of some of the animals in the zoo. I took myself off to see 'Mamma Mia' at the theatre for my last night in London. I loved it, but then I love anything with Abba music.

The following two weeks were spent on the south coast in the town of Hastings. This was the town I had earmarked to buy a flat for my retirement, so I wanted to know if I would like it enough to live there one day. I managed to find a little holiday flat under an art gallery, in the Old Town part of Hastings. I fell in love with the old town. It was exactly the sort of place I was looking for. Plenty of history and architecture. Some of the homes dated back to the thirteenth century. Oodles of quaint shops and restaurants, and no less than fifteen old pubs just in the old town. This was what I had in mind. While I was there, Britain had the most snow it had seen in thirty years.

Everywhere I went, it was like a postcard scene with everything covered in snow. Up on the grasslands on the hills that flank the old town, families were tobogganing down the slopes. Even the little street opposite my flat was being used by people with snow sleds. Children had built a family of snowmen in the church grounds opposite me. I took them some carrots to use for noses, and provided a hat and scarf for 'mama' snowlady. Of course, Alfie joined in with the frivolities. The children loved him and I took many photos. I even had a ride in their sled, over what I later discovered was gravestones.

It was such a perfect setting, I was reminded of the movie 'Funny Farm' with Chevy Chase where he buys an old farm to spend his days writing his book. But everything goes wrong with the house, so he decides to sell up. He pays the town folk to 'pretend' they live in some magical village all covered in snow, with deer roaming and everything appearing picture perfect, to entice buyers to his home. Was this what was happening here in Hastings? I amused myself with that thought.

Whether my sanity had been affected by my heartbreak I don't know, but having Alfie with me proved to be a great comfort. In the same way that people talk to their pets, I would arrive home after a days outing and 'talk' to Alfie. He was always either sitting on the lounge, or in bed waiting for me. This is what my life had reduced to - the only bedmate I had was a stuffed monkey! Mind you, it was so much quieter than having George around and we never argued. The sex left a little to be desired!

During the long nights in the flat, I kept myself occupied by knitting - for Alfie. He didn't have enough warm clothes I had decided. So I found a wool shop in town and agonised over what colour I thought he would like. I knitted him a scarf, beanie and boots in multi blue colours with a black band around the edge of the beanie and boots. He looked very smart. I then walked my feet off looking for new clothes, settling on a red top and blue striped overalls from the baby department of Marks and Spencers. With leftover wool I made a pair of ski pants and a vest. I was happy, he now had enough warm clothes. Of course Lisa did point out to me that he did have his own layer of fur to keep him warm. But it was snowing and freezing - she didn't understand.

It was during these two weeks that I found out George was staying not far from me, less than an hour's drive. I sent him a very brief email saying that it was eating away at me that he was so close, and couldn't he find it within himself to just meet up with me? I deserved an explanation. Every night I'd go to sleep working out another scenario of what might have happened. It was driving me crazy, I had to know the truth. He emailed me on my last morning in Hastings saying he had no transport, but would try and meet me at Windsor where I was spending my last couple of days.

I flew over to Dublin and was met by a family I didn't know. My daughter's friend and her mum and dad, they were the most welcoming people I've ever known. They took it in turns of showing me around, I met the rest of the family and their spouses. I had a delightful time with them. I spent a day in Dublin, being dropped off and picked up at the train station. The youngest brother spent his day off work, showing me the countryside and treating me to lunch. The older sister had just had her first baby and spent most of her time at her mum's, so I spent time with a tiny new baby. I travelled over to Derry and spent a night there. Then on to Belfast for my last night. What a delightful Irish family. And they all loved Alfie. He was bigger than the baby!

On the day of my departure, they presented me with a magnificent book on County Antrim. It was gorgeous - they had marked all the places they had shown me. What a lovely thoughtful gift, what lovely people. Although all I could think about when I picked it up was "Bugger, this is going to put my suitcase over weight". I was flying on one of those discount airlines who are really strict about weight, I'd already posted some of my stuff onto Liverpool to lighten the load. It did put my case overweight- it cost me forty pounds in excess baggage!

Onto Liverpool for a couple of days. Did the Magical Mystery Tour and the ferry across the Mersey - with Alfie. Again, lots of photos and again, he stole the limelight. He was a great people-meeter I had discovered. Curious isn't it? People hardly ever talk to you if you are alone, but the moment I produced a stuffed animal out of a bag, I had new friends. I met up with Lauren's sister and hubby and had a wonderful couple of days with them, enjoying a pub crawl in their daughter's locale and high tea in the classy Hard Days Night hotel where I viewed some amazing Beatles memorabilia. I also stumbled across the Spanish restaurant that George and I had dined in on that last trip and enjoyed some fabulous tapas.

Derby was my next port of call, to see my friends from Ibiza. It was wonderful catching up with them again, it had only been seven months since we met. What a cad they thought George was. They were shocked, they were planning on coming to our wedding! We'd joked with them about getting married in Vegas, with them as our bridesmaid and best man. I don't know what they were more disappointed with - us breaking up or missing out on a trip to Vegas! We had a great time though reminiscing together.

I stayed in Derby a couple of days and explored this lovely town with it's huge Westfield shopping centre. I visited their beautiful cathedral, wandering around inside taking photographs and wondering why many people were walking inside very dressed up. I had walked into the start of a funeral! I took myself off to an interesting museum of Rolls Royce engines - it was actually quite fascinating seeing aeroplane engines up close, they were huge.

I had told Donna about George maybe meeting up with me in Windsor the next day. She hoped I didn't, it would just stir up emotions again she said. I deserved better, they felt. We said our goodbyes, she gave me a copy of 'Eat, Pray, Love' to help me heal and I left them to mind my lovely warm coat and a pair of gumboots I had purchased for the snow, as well as more warm clothes. I couldn't fit them in my suitcase (now with the extra book), and I was planning to come back to live for a while in April or May if things worked out.

The following day I travelled down to Windsor to stay the night and visit the castle on my last day. My flight didn't leave till night time and Windsor is not far from Heathrow airport. So it was a good way to finish my trip, I'd always wanted to visit the castle. I had emailed George before I went to Ireland, giving him details of where I was staying and how I planned to see Windsor Castle on that last day. Could he try and fit in a couple of hours, I had asked him. I gave him my UK phone number.

I checked my emails before I left Derby, as I did every day. But my hotel in Windsor didn't have free internet. I spent the night having dinner in a lovely riverside restaurant. The next morning, I was late leaving for the castle and didn't bother checking my emails at the hotel lobby. I'll check them when I return from the castle, I thought. If George was going to meet me, he would call or message me.

I spent a lovely day touring the castle, it was magnificent. During a tour in the bowels of the kitchen wing, there was an evacuation siren. Not a practice drill, the real thing. Given the extensive damage of the 1992 fire, they took this seriously. We were all herded into a quadrangle where I snuck a photo of a prohibited section of the grounds, through an arch to the 'Long Walk'. Trust me to be caught up in a drama! I spent longer than I had planned in there, so raced back to my hotel to grab my suitcase and made my way by bus to the airport. After I checked my case through, I had time to go check my emails.

There was an email from George - sent at six that morning. Saying he would meet me in Windsor around three that afternoon and could drive me to the airport. I had missed his email! The first day of my entire trip that I hadn't checked my emails. I checked my phone - no messages. I then discovered I had given him a wrong number, I had mixed two numbers back to front. So he couldn't reach me by phone either.

I had missed my chance of seeing him. Of hearing his explanation.

The universe really does work in mysterious ways, I thought. It had found a way to spare me the pain of meeting up with him. It knew I was still too emotionally raw to face him, just as my friend had said. I wasn't meant to see him again.

My roller coaster ride was finally over. The engine had run out of steam.

Chapter 27

Whirling Dervishes and Hershey Bars

As planned, on my return I commenced work at a new office. My daughter had already been there since before I left so was well established and doing very well. I couldn't settle, my heart just wasn't in it.

I had already decided while I was away that I would move over to Hastings for six months to try and buy a flat to keep for my retirement. This would entail securing a job there - I was confidant I could, having spoken to some agencies whilst I was there in January. So I was just filling in time in this new office, really.

I moved into my investment home on my return from the UK, again as planned. It was a mess, my tenant had left it in a disgusting state, and ten weeks behind in her rent. I gave myself a month to renovate it and put it on the market. My plan was to return to Hastings late April or early May in time for their summer. I had just enough funds to pay for the renovations and survive until it sold.

This decision all came about because of George and his dropping out of my life. I had been wanting to experience living either in Spain, France or England for some years, but abandoned the idea when I thought that he was coming to live in Australia with me. I mentioned to him in my final email how strange it is that something good always comes out of a bad situation. I was going to live my dream.

Renovations happened at a rapid rate. It was hard work, some of the jobs I did myself. I had to have the entire house repainted, there were holes in walls, doors kicked in, a window broken and every wall and ceiling covered in nicotine. I had the timber floors sanded and polished - they looked fantastic. The toilets had to be replaced, they were so filthy. A handyman fixed all the odd problems. I cleaned up the gardens. Exactly one month to the day of moving in, the house went on the market.

During this month of renovating, I had met up with an old friend for dinner one night. My friend who's son had passed away four years previous. We had stayed in touch, he now lived on the Gold Coast. He proceeded to tell me about a trip he was taking the next month with his new lady. He was flying to Los Angeles, spending a week in Las Vegas, going on a cruise in the Caribbean then onto New York. The exact same trip I was meant to be doing with George with my free business class tickets. Of course, he was doing it in style - staying at the Bellagio in Vegas, a luxury yacht for the cruise and staying at the Waldorf hotel in New York. His lucky lady, I thought to myself. I told him my story of how I won my tickets, and now had to abandon the whole trip because of George. And a lack of funds. I couldn't justify spending the money while I was renovating my house. John got a bit cross with me about letting such a fabulous prize go. He pointed out that it was bad enough that George wasn't going to go with me, but I would never forgive myself for losing such a valuable prize for the sake of a small amount of money. Which I would have as soon as my house sold. He offered to pay for my trip.

I laughed the offer off, I couldn't accept that sort of thing. The next day I had drinks with the girls and told them of his generous offer that I had dismissed. Go for it, they told me. "You're going to be bitter and angry for the rest of your life that that cad of a man caused you to forfeit this trip. If your friend has offered to help you out, you should graciously accept his kind offer. He wouldn't have made it if he didn't care about you" they told me in unison. I agreed with them about being bitter and angry, I was already feeling that way. And it would only be a matter of weeks before I could pay my friend back. I rang John that night and the money was in my account two days later. "Book somewhere nice, not trashy" he told me. He gave me more than I had needed. "Just make sure you have a great time, to spite that man" he laughed.

And so, with just over a week till my departure date, I phoned the airline to tell them I was still going but to cancel the other ticket. Gosh, I am blessed with wonderful friends, I told myself. And everyone else.

With my bargain hunting skills, I managed to book a popular hotel in Vegas right in the centre of the 'Strip' for a minimal price, found a fantastic cruise around the Caribbean for a week at a hugely discounted rate, booked air tickets between Los Angeles, Las Vegas, Miami and New York and secured a boutique hotel right in Times Square. I had become a master at last minute internet bookings.

I was off, again. I calculated that in three months, I had only worked four weeks. I could get used to this, if only it paid well!

I had to break the news to my new boss. "Well, it's like this…."

He was great about it, would have done the exact same thing, he told me.

First stop Dubai for a two day stopover. This had been previously booked as it broke up two sixteen hour flights - a long time even in business class. I was thrilled to find a young girl had been upgraded to George's empty seat. She was a 'volunteer' who would forfeit her seat if someone needed one urgently, and would wait till she could be allocated a new flight. She had done this on a number of occasions and as a reward for her generosity, they upgraded her to business class. So the two of us were like kids in a toy shop, playing with all the gadgets and lapping up the extra attention. Champagne while we waited for the passengers to be seated - lovely. And yes please, I would love some canapé's while we wait for take off.

I was finally able to do the 'camel safari, barbecue in a Bedouin camp' trip that I had missed out on previously because I was ill. I had no problem going alone, I was so used to it. It was really enjoyable. Great entertainment, I finally found out what a 'whirling dervish' was - a dancer who twirls around in circles in a circular skirt, it was a great spectacle. The following day I visited the Mall of the Emirates, wow what a beautiful shopping centre. Had a look at the ski centre they had built there - a snowfield in the middle of a desert. I then took myself out to 'Atlantis', the new multi billion dollar resort. I had planned to go into the water park, but was so mesmerized with the hotel itself, that I spent the day in there. I'd never seen anything so opulent, it was dripping with riches. The aquarium was out of this world, with huge viewing panels inside the hotel. A whole Atlantis world underwater, it was incredible. I had a beautiful lunch in an Italian restaurant, one of many in the resort. I sent John a text message "if you ever come to Dubai, you have to stay in Atlantis, its amazing", I said to him. "I'll keep it in mind" he replied. I had drinks and dinner in a rooftop bar that night, overlooking the city. There were comfy lounges and beds with canopies strewn around the rooftop, very bizarre. Lovely atmosphere though.

Another great flight to Los Angeles. I boarded an internal flight straight to Las Vegas, I had no wish to stay in LA, I'd been there once before. That was enough.

My hotel was wonderful, close to all the main casinos, all the big names. Caesars Palace and Bellagio were just across the road. The casino in my hotel was huge, and very popular. I was given discount vouchers and free play money on my arrival. The Strip was a hive of activity, I wandered along its length after enjoying a healthy salad for dinner at the top of the Eiffel Tower casino. This was going to be a fun four days, there was entertainment everywhere.

The following morning, I couldn't manage anything for breakfast, just a juice. I felt a little off colour. I returned to my room to prepare to head out for the day, and was struck by another bout of vomiting and diarrhoea. Oh no, not again! This couldn't happen to me twice, surely. It did. What was it this time, I wondered. Couldn't have been the food on the flight, it was fabulous. The only thing I could put it down to was the meat at the barbecue, it had probably been sitting in the heat of the desert all day before we ate it. Whatever it was, I was a mess. All day I threw up and raced to the toilet. It lasted three days out of the four. Even my room maid was concerned about me, she saw how bad I looked. She supplied me with glasses of ice cubes, it was all I could manage. Again, I was so weak I had to keep going back to bed.

I would venture out to one of the famous casinos for a short visit, then straight back to bed. No food for three days. My jeans became so loose on me, I had to wear a belt. I had booked a trip to the Grand Canyon and had to cancel it at midnight, it was a fourteen hour day that I was in no condition to endure. I had now visited every ladies room in every posh hotel in Las Vegas - I could write a report on the subject. I did manage to sit through a couple of shows on my third and last nights, which I enjoyed. I had to report back to John. "No, I didn't get laid in Vegas. I was not a pretty sight."

Next stop, Miami, to board my ship. Fortunately, I had recovered from my recent bout of stomach bug, just in time to gorge myself with food on the cruise. Same cruise line as my previous cruise with Angie, different ship. Again, it was beautiful. I was thrilled with my cabin. I had been told to expect a small cabin with bunk beds as my booking was so last minute. To my surprise, it was spacious with a queen size bed and no overhead bunks. No window, but on the outside of the ship just under the anchor, so right at the front. If it hit anything at sea, I'd be the first to know about it, I laughed to myself.

The cruise was wonderful and very therapeutic for me. It visited Nassau in the Bahamas, St Thomas in the Virgin Islands, San Juan in Puerto Rico - I looked everywhere for any sign of Ricco, and Grand Turk in the Turks and Cacos Islands. It wasn't very grand, I wondered what Little Turk must have looked like. I swam on a beach in the Bahamas and visited the famous Hard Rock Cafe, went snorkelling in St Thomas, paddled in the sea in Puerto Rico. I met some lovely people, my dinner mates were a family from Alaska who were delightful. The entertainment was much more professional than my last cruise experience. Enjoyed a great St Patrick's day party on board the ship.

I stayed overnight in Miami in a hotel in the famous South Beach area. Famous for its Art Deco hotels. What this translated to in reality was old, dirty and run down hotels that needed a complete re-furb. Or a bull-dozer. I was greeted after my return from dinner by a young man being interrogated by police in the hallway near my room. Later it was the girlfriends turn, giving her teary recount of the night's proceedings. I made sure I latched my door. The restaurant strip was full of interesting characters, much like you would expect to see in Miami. Didn't do anything for me, it was just an exaggerated version of Surfer's Paradise on a Saturday night. Or perhaps I'm just getting old?

New York, New York. I loved New York. It was everything you see on television. Flashing lights, yellow cabs, swarms of people and a wonderful vibe about it. My hotel was right in Times Square, with Broadway theatres in my street. Will Smith and his wife were appearing in a play next door to me, Niles from Frasier was in another play, and Catherine Zeta Jones and Angela Lansbury were starring in 'A Little Night Music' around the corner. I decided to see this play, I admire Miss Zeta Jones for her versatility. She was brilliant, I thoroughly enjoyed the play. I couldn't go to Broadway and not go to the theatre, I decided. Again it was made memorable - they had to stop the play in the second act - someone in the front rows was having a heart attack! When the leading man called "Is there a doctor in the house?" he wasn't joking! It could only happen to me, I mused to myself.

I discovered the Hershey store, on a corner in Times Square. I fell in love with their chocolate and peanut butter bars, similar to a bon bon sweet I used to make at Christmas time. I returned every day to buy more chocolate. I bought some to take home for my girls. They didn't make it home. Well, Australia does have strict quarantine rules about bringing food in, doesn't it?

I did the usual touristy things, rode the hop on, hop off bus around for two days, did a night tour of Brooklyn. The views back to the city were stunning. I visited the site of the World Trade Centre and saw the murals everywhere. And of course caught the ferry to Ellis Island to view the Statue of Liberty. It was a bit of a whirlwind tour, just a sampler of the city. I will be back, I decided.

I had a limousine transfer to the airport, courtesy of my prize and was collected by a delightful driver from Morocco. He tried to convince me that Morocco was where I should be considering buying an investment property, not England. He very kindly stopped at Central Park and took some photos of me. I hadn't had a chance to explore the park in my three days there. I took a photo of him, he had a beautiful smile. We exchanged email addresses. He gave me a kiss at the airport. Mmmm, a handsome Moroccan living in New York. Who was retiring to Morocco in a few years. That could be tempting.

Ahhh, I think I was finally getting over George.

The End

****

EPILOGUE

My investment house sold within a week of going on the market, while I was vomiting in Las Vegas. Nicole negotiated the deal for me, she had power of attorney over me and was able to sign my contract. Settlement wasn't for eight weeks, I would have five weeks after I returned from my trip to get myself organised for England.

As it happened, I discovered there was a festival happening in Hastings on May Day weekend that I didn't want to miss. It was very pagan, with people dressing up in weird and wonderful outfits, culminating in a ritual of 'slaying' a character to welcome in the summer, up in the ruins of the old castle. I was able to bring settlement of my house forward by two weeks by offering to pay the buyers rent for that time. It was actually an advantage to me economically, I saved more on the interest on my mortgage than the cost of their rent.

So I flew out on a Saturday, arrived Sunday and witnessed the festival on Monday. And wouldn't have missed it for the world. It was outrageously weird, nothing like anything we had back in Australia - we just don't have the history.

I mysteriously found a flat to rent in the Old Town, exactly where I wanted to be. It was on the top floor of a fifteenth century house that used to be an old pub. It had amazing views of the sea and the fishing fleet to the front, and the hills and castle to the rear. I settled in and loved every minute of my stay there.

While I waited for my flat to be ready - it was being repainted and having new carpet laid before I moved in - I took myself off to Mallorca, Spain for five days, it worked out cheaper than driving around the countryside staying in bed and breakfasts.

As for George, yes I did hear from him. He knew that I was now living in Hastings, so contacted me and asked if I wanted to meet up with him for some 'closure'. He would understand if I didn't.

Damn right I did. I wanted to see him squirm. We arranged to meet in Brighton (neutral territory, I thought). I wore the sexiest dress I had, I wanted to show him what he had given up! I found him sitting at our meeting place and he was very sheepish to begin with. He didn't know how I would react, he said. I think he was worried I'd produce a knife or something. I did *really* want to slap him, just to make me feel better. I refrained. Too many people around. "You can do all the talking" I said to him "you have some explaining to do, don't you?"

He did do some explaining. It was true about the ten year ban, the authorities wanted names of people in Australia who had aided him in staying there without a visa. Of course he refused to name them, so they slapped the ban on him. He didn't know what to do about me. Felt that if we married, everyone would assume it was just for entry into Australia. I pointed out to him that by him dumping me, *that* looked like he was only with me for entry into Australia, which had now been quashed. He tried reconciling with Jane, that didn't work out. He was now living with his daughter and her partner in Dubai. Never once in the conversation did he say "I'm sorry" to me.

There was no tugging at the heartstrings for me this time. I left him feeling happy that I'd had this chance, but ready to move on. He'd caused me too much pain and hurt to want to continue with him. And he was too irresponsible. We said our goodbyes. It was over.

Again, I was reminded of that line from an email:

'Don't cry because it's over, smile because it happened.'

I had *plenty* to smile about.